To Esther and Joe,
with best wishes,

Philip Mosley

Bruges-la-Morte

Sept. 08

GEORGES RODENBACH

BRUGES-LA-MORTE

—ROMAN—

Frontispice de Fernand Khnopff et 35 Illustrations

PARIS
LIBRAIRIE MARPON & FLAMMARION
E. FLAMMARION, SUCC^r

26, RUE RACINE, PRÈS L'ODÉON

Bruges-la-Morte

a novel

By

Georges Rodenbach
Translated from the French with an Introduction
by Philip Mosley

University of Scranton Press
Scranton and London

Library of Congress Cataloging-in-Publication Data

Rodenbach, Georges, 1855–1898.
[Bruges-la-Morte. English]
Bruges-la-Morte: a novel / by Georges Rodenbach;
translated from the French by Philip Mosley.
p. cm.
Includes bibliographical references and index.
ISBN 978-1-58966-159-2 (pbk.: alk. paper)
I. Mosley, Philip. II. Title.
PQ2388.R413B713 2007
843'.8—dc22

2007034261

Distribution:

The University of Scranton Press
Chicago Distribution Center
11030 S. Langley
Chicago, IL 60628

Contents

Acknowledgements

This translation of *Bruges-la-Morte*, the first in English since Thomas Duncan's 1903 version, was published originally in 1986 by Wilfion Books in Paisley, Scotland, and again in 1987 jointly with Dufour Editions in Chester Springs, Pennsylvania. Those editions are out of print. I am therefore grateful to Jeff Gainey, Director of the University of Scranton Press, for his willingness to make this translation available again in a new edition. I am also grateful to Konrad Hopkins, Director of Wilfion Books, for kindly permitting this edition to be published. The cover illustration, *Pandora's Box* (1951), by René Magritte, is reproduced by kind permission of Yale University Art Gallery. Fernand Khnopff's frontispiece for the original edition of *Bruges-la-Morte* (1892) is reproduced by kind permission of the Archives and Museum of Literature, Brussels.

Introduction
by
Philip Mosley

Georges Rodenbach was born on 16 July 1855 at Tournai, Belgium. In November of that year, the Rodenbach family moved to Ghent, where young Georges was brought up and educated, first at the *Ecole moyenne*, then at the Collège Sainte-Barbe, and lastly at the University of Ghent, where he read Law. Other notable literary figures educated at Sainte-Barbe were Emile Verhaeren, Charles Van Lerberghe, Grégoire Le Roy, and Maurice Maeterlinck.

Rodenbach began his literary career in 1876 with the publication of a sonnet, "Fidelity," in a Brussels magazine. With his friend Verhaeren, whom he had met at the Collège Sainte-Barbe, he frequented a Catholic literary salon in Ghent, reading his poetry there. In 1877, his first collection of poems, *Le Foyer et les champs*, was published, attracting praise from the Catholic press.

Graduating as Doctor of Law, Rodenbach went to the Bar in Ghent. Pursuing a family tradition, however, he was sent by his father to Paris for a probationary period, and while there, he attended the theater, contributed to such magazines as *La Plume* and *La Jeune France*, and became acquainted with Hugo, Coppée and de Banville. Between November 1878 and June 1879, twenty-one of his 'Parisian Letters' appeared in the Brussels weekly *La Paix*.

A second volume of poems, *Les Tristesses*, was published in Paris, and one of the poems in it, 'Le Coffret' ('The Casket'), quickly became famous. When he returned to Ghent in July 1879, Rodenbach complained in a letter to Verhaeren, revealing both genuine frustration with his native culture and a somewhat shortsighted view of the potential of Belgian writing:

> I am out of my element, sad, lost, woebegone. To go in for literature in Belgium, in my opinion, is useless and impossible.

Nonetheless, within two years, Rodenbach—along with Max Waller, Emile Verhaeren, Max Elskamp, Maurice Maeterlinck, and Charles Van Lerberghe—was involved in a Belgian literary revival, which demonstrated the existence of a vital strain of Belgian writing as well as a degree of resistance to the hegemony of Parisian culture.

Perhaps the most potent symbol of this revival was the review *La Jeune Belgique* ('Young Belgium'), published from 1 December 1881 to 25 December 1897. The Young Belgium movement was not consciously nationalistic, though it had something of that effect on its observers. Its ideology was aesthetic not nationalistic, yet its aesthetics for the most part failed to transcend the literary conventions of the day. According to a statement by Edmond Picard, an older writer and lawyer, and co-founder of the radical review *L'Art moderne*, in the issue of 12 January 1890:

> Art has in our time assumed an aristocratic aspect. It has gradually drawn away from the masses.... It exists only for a few who call themselves the elite.... A scornful sort of shibboleth has entered into circulation, born of anger at not being understood except by the finer spirits: the artist should produce works only for the rare species of the highly cultivated....

The response of Rodenbach and some other writers to Picard's call for a committed national and political literature was dismissive of such ideals. Even so, in 1883, Rodenbach had made a fiery speech at a banquet given by *La Jeune Belgique* in honour of his fellow Belgian author Camille Lemonnier, in which he declared:

> This banquet is not only a celebration—it's also the launching of an offensive. In a way, it's the eve of a battle for a group of fully committed conscripts who come, at this solemn hour, to greet you and salute you as their literary Field-Marshal.

Only three years later, in 1886, Rodenbach (together with Lemonnier and Verhaeren) dissociated himself from the ultra-aestheticism of those of his contemporaries who followed Max Waller and Albert Giraud.

Having become partner in Edmond Picard's law practice in 1883, Rodenbach settled in Brussels, but continued to publish a variety of literary works until 1886, when he stepped down from the Bar and thereafter devoted himself entirely to writing.

A third volume of poems, *La Mer élégante*, was published in 1881, and a fourth one, *L'Hiver mondain*, came out in 1884, as did *La Petite Veuve*, a one-act prose sketch written in collaboration with Max Waller. Of another collection of poems, *La Jeunesse blanche* (1886), Rodenbach's biographer, Pierre Maes, remarked that it was 'a moment of happy balance between Parnassian rigidity and the excessive looseness of the early symbolists.' In the same year, his first novel, *La Vie morte*, was serialized in *L'Indépendance belge*.

By 1888, Rodenbach had left Belgium and settled permanently in Paris, having taken up an appointment as correspondent for the *Journal de Bruxelles*, in which he published his weekly 'Parisian Letters' until 1895. In August 1888, he married Anna-Maria Urbain (1860–1945). They had one son, Constantin, who was born in 1892, the year in which *Bruges-la-Morte* was published.

Between 1888 and 1892, Rodenbach's publications included an article, 'Agonies de villes,' dedicated to Bruges; a short story 'L'Amour en exil'; *Du silence*, a collection of poems; *L'Art en exil*, a novel, which was a reworked version of *La Vie morte*; and a further collection of poems, *Le Règne du silence*. But it was *Bruges-la-Morte* that established Rodenbach's fame and fixed his reputation as a master of symbolist fiction.

First published by Marpon and Flammarion, in Paris, with a frontispiece by the Belgian artist Fernand Khnopff and thirty-five photographic illustrations, *Bruges-la-Morte* was the most successful French literary publication of 1892, with the possible exception of the play *Pelléas et Mélisande* by Maurice Maeterlinck, an important symbolist text, which did not, however, have the immediate impact of Rodenbach's work. Emile Verhaeren wrote of the novel: 'Rodenbach sang the praises of Bruges because of all cities in the world he considered it most in tune with his sense of melancholy.... Bruges is the book's protagonist and nothing better explains the novel or tells us more about the poet himself....'

Bruges-la-Morte is a love story—Rodenbach calls it a 'study of passion'—not only the author's love for the novel's 'protagonist,' the city of Bruges, but also the obsessive love of the human protagonist, Hugues Viane, for his dead wife, of whom he has made an almost religious cult centered on a tress of her hair as a kind of holy relic. In his mind, he discerns similarities between the dead woman and the 'dead city,' to such a degree that he can imagine that 'Bruges was his wife, while she was Bruges.'

An even more striking similarity and identification appears in the fatally attractive young theatrical dancer Jane Scott, who bears an uncanny resemblance—a 'demon of resemblance,' says Rodenbach—to Hugues's lost wife. Deluding himself that his wife has returned to him in the dancer's lithe form, Hugues transfers his obsessive passion to Jane, whose true nature—vulgar, avaricious and shallow—is slowly revealed to him. When she desecrates the tress of hair, Hugues, in a rage, strangles her with it, and in the stillness after the murder, Bruges, his other love, *Bruges-la-Morte*, reasserts its powerful hold on him as the church bells ring out again over deserted streets and silent canals in plangent sounds like the listless shedding of 'petals of flowers of iron.'

Rodenbach never lived in Bruges, although it was both his father's and grandfather's home town. Joris-Karl Huysmans, in his essay on Bruges, touches on Rodenbach's family attachment to that city, which, he says, 'belongs to him, has become, so to speak, his dowry, and the view of it, even when he is not speaking about it specifically, looms up behind all his novels and poems.' Rodenbach himself confirmed his attachment to the city in a letter written in 1894 to the Bruges critic Arthur Daxhelet: 'There is atavism in works of art, and heredity also explains my love for the admirable Bruges, which I'd be happy to have assured a little glory in the French (*sic*) artistic mind.' This combination of family connection and kindred spirit enabled Rodenbach to conceive of Bruges as identical to his own temperament, for, as he writes in the novel, 'every city is a state of mind.' To Rodenbach, Bruges was an ideal city of art, an inspiring blend of the real and the fabulous. Much more than Ghent, where he had grown up, it was a city in accord with his melancholic feelings.

Rodenbach was keenly aware of the contrast between Bruges and Ghent, in spite of the clear historical parallels. Ghent had also experienced what he calls 'that inexorable fatality' in its decline from medieval power and grandeur. But unlike Bruges after the 15th century, Ghent had never resigned itself to the slow decay that had the effect of enhancing the medieval beauty of Bruges. Ghent, on the contrary, had become infused with the artistic and commercial spirit of northern Flanders, best exemplified by the great port-city of Antwerp.

Rodenbach's novel *L'Art en exil* (1889), set in Ghent, concerns a highly refined artist, Jean Rembrandt, who desperately tries to resist the materialism and philistinism of the province. It anticipates *Bruges-la-Morte* both in its fatalism and its treatment of the city as an influential force, a place that almost assumes the status of a character, although it is less romanticized than in the later novel. The romanticized image of Bruges overshadows the facts of the city in its prime. It was not a quiet, picturesque haven, but a bustling, industrial city where rich and poor were equally subject to its rigorous practices of manufacture and marketing.

In another novel, *Le Carillonneur* (1897), the protagonist Joris Borluut finds peace and quiet in the Bruges belfry, where, in the end, having been humiliated by the successful endeavors to modernize the city, he hangs himself by the very bell-rope which symbolizes his allegiance to Bruges. Blending realism with symbolism, *Le Carillonneur* is Rodenbach's most convincing work of fiction, both plot and characterization having greater depth and credibility than elsewhere in his novels and short stories. Although it also tells of a death in Bruges, it stands at a curious tangent to the more lyrical and renowned *Bruges-la-Morte.*

Just as Rodenbach acknowledged in *Bruges-la-Morte* the heritage of the great Flemish painters Hans

Memling and Jan van Eyck, and their descendants, so did *Bruges-la-Morte* itself inspire French and Belgian artists to illustrate the various editions of the novel. The first edition (1892) carried a Fernand Khnopff frontispiece that we have included in this edition. It depicts an Ophelia-like figure floating in a canal. The 1900 edition contained forty-three woodcuts by Henri Paillard, the 1910 edition included work by Marin Baldo, and the 1919 edition had a portrait of Rodenbach by J.–F. Raffaëlli. But the mood and spirit of the novel were most effectively expressed in the 1930 editon, which was enhanced with eighteen original pastels by the French symbolist artist Lucien Lévy-Dhurmer, who (in 1896) also rendered a distinctive portrait of Rodenbach, showing him tousled and with a melancholic look in his eyes, standing on the Quai des Marbriers in Bruges, his body seeming to dissolve imperceptibly into the dark canal behind him.

No other artist, however, captured Rodenbach's mood of solitary introspection better than Fernand Khnopff, who once observed that his soul was alone and free from influence, like glass enclosed in silence, a figure that recalls Rodenbach's equally hermetic image in the quotation that serves as the epigraph to this translation of *Bruges-la-Morte:*

Thus my soul alone, and which nothing influences: it is as if enclosed in glass and in silence, given over entire to its own interior spectacle.

As Hubert Juin has pointed out, the affinity between Khnopff and Rodenbach is evident in their common interests, which he names as 'the identity of summoned women, the sadness of cities inexorably doomed to shipwreck, the nostalgia of what is, or has become, inaccessible.'

Khnopff's drawing *Une Ville abandonnée* ('An Abandoned City') (1904), exactly illustrates a line from one of Rodenbach's poems: 'In the deserted squares of joyless cities.' In Khnopff's drawing the city square is the Hans Memling Square in Bruges, with a central statue removed from its plinth and the sea encroaching from the right side. The dreamlike, silent emptiness of the scene creates an eerie, ominous atmosphere that reflects the ambiance and feeling of desolation in *Bruges-la-Morte*.

The novel was also one of the sources of the opera *Die tote Stadt* ('The Dead City') by Erich Wolfgang Korngold (1897–1957) and was filmed as *Brugge, die Stille* ('Bruges the Silent'), produced in Belgium in 1981. Directed by Roland Verhavert from a screenplay by him and the film critic Théodore Louis, and with music by Claude Debussy, the color film was praised by Paul Davay for its 'considerable plastic beauty.' But, he went on to say, 'this story of a man obsessed with his religious scruples has left Belgian audiences cold, especially the younger generation.'

Rodenbach adapted *Bruges-la-Morte* into a four-act play, *Le Mirage*, which was published posthumously, first in the *Revue de Paris* in April 1900 and then as a book in 1901. At the suggestion of Rodenbach's widow, *Le Mirage* was translated into German by the Viennese playwright and poet Siegfried Trebitsch. First published with the title *Die stille Stadt* in 1902, then as *Das Trugbild* in 1913, this version was staged at least once, in 1903, at the Lessing Theatre in Berlin. According to Trebitsch in an article on Rodenbach, he later 'met the young master Erich Wolfgang Korngold in search of a scenario or even better, a mood or operatic background which would be dramatically elaborated. I urged him to take up the "Trugbild".'

The composer's father, Dr. Julius Korngold, music critic of the important Vienna journal *Neue Freie Presse*, offered the play to Hans Müller, a Viennese author who had been the librettist of Korngold's earlier one-act opera *Violanta*, to prepare the libretto. When his treatment proved to be unsatisfactory, however, Dr. Korngold collaborated with his son in writing their own libretto under the pen-name Paul Schott, in the process making some changes in the plot and characters of Rodenbach's novel and play, most notably the interpolation of a dream sequence in which the dancer is murdered. The younger Korngold composed the music for the three-act opera between 1916 and 1920.

Simultaneously premièred in Hamburg and Cologne on 4 December 1920, *Die tote Stadt* was afterwards performed in some eighty opera houses throughout Europe and, in an English version, at the Metropolitan Opera in New York in its 1921–1922 season. 'A happy coincidence,' wrote Trebitsch, made it possible for Rodenbach's son Constantin to be in Vienna at the time of the opera's première there, 'and to attend the performance and the revival of his father's fame, for the musical feat of the young master will erect a permanent memorial to the dead poet.'

In the 1930s, however, because Korngold was Jewish, Hitler had the opera removed from the authorized repertoire. After the Second World War, in the 1960s, it reappeared on European opera stages. Revived in New York in 1975, it was also recorded, under the direction of Erich Leinsdorf, and in February 1983 it was staged again in a controversial and very successful production by the Deutsche Oper Berlin, which has since established the work in its repertoire. One interesting feature of the Berlin production is that the set (designed by Andreas Reinhardt) for Act II is a replica of the Hans Memling Square in Bruges as depicted in Khnopff's

Une Ville abandonnée, complete with the empty plinth and the encroaching sea (real water on stage). Following further revivals of *Die tote Stadt* in Europe and North America, Georges Rodenbach and *Bruges-la-Morte*, for ever linked with Korngold's work, are inevitably mentioned and often discussed in the press coverage of the opera, which has certainly become a 'permanent memorial' to both the man and his novel.

From 1895, Rodenbach suffered from a serious chest complaint as well as neurasthenia, and his health deteriorated rapidly. On 24 December 1898, he died of typhlitis in Paris, aged forty-three, and was buried four days later in Père-Lachaise Cemetery.

Other works by Rodenbach were published, some of them posthumously (see the Chronology of his Works), after *Bruges-la-Morte*, but none enjoyed the sensational success of that novel, which has continued to be issued in French-language editions and has also been translated into several other languages.

The first English translation (in 1903) was by Thomas Duncan, who took a number of liberties with the text. In the present version, the translator has attempted to be faithful both to the letter and the spirit of Rodenbach's original text, which is generally recognized as a major work of francophone Belgian writing and of the symbolist movement.

Rodenbach may not have achieved any radical technical or conceptual breakthrough in fiction, but he did, nevertheless, make a substantial contribution to the developing aesthetics of post-Romantic literature, and for this reason alone *Bruges-la-Morte* deserves to be remembered and read. Although sometimes seeming melodramatic and sentimental, this novel remains Rodenbach's most celebrated and most captivating work, the definitive eulogy to an old Flemish 'dead city' that frames the haunting story of a haunted love.

Chronology of Works by Georges Rodenbach (1855–1898)

1877. *Le Foyer et les champs* ('The Hearth and the Fields'). A collection of poems.

1879. *Les Tristesses* ('The Sorrows'). A collection of poems.

1880. *La Belgique*. A historical poem.

1881. *La Mer élégante* ('The Elegant Sea'). A collection of poems.

1884. *L'Hiver mondain* ('The Worldly Winter'). A collection of poems.

1884. *La Petite Veuve* ('The Little Widow'), with Max Waller. A one-act prose sketch.

1886. *La Jeunesse blanche* ('The Whiteness of Youth'). A collection of poems.

1886. *La Vie morte* ('The Dead Life'). A novel.

1887. *Le Livre de Jésus* ('The Book of Jesus'). A collection of poems, unfinished. Published in part in 1923.

1888. 'L'Amour en exil' ('Love in Exile'). A short story.

1888. *Du silence* ('Of Silence'). A collection of poems.

1889. *L'Art en exil* ('Art in Exile'). A novel, a reworked version of *La Vie morte*.

1891. *Le Règne du silence* ('The Reign of Silence'). A collection of poems, incorporating a reprint of *Du silence*.

1892. *Bruges-la-Morte*. A novel.

1893. *Le Voyage dans les yeux* ('Journey into the Eyes'). A collection of poems.

1894. *Le Voile* ('The Veil'). A one-act verse play.

1894. *Musée de béguines* ('Museum of Beguines'). Still-life portraits and short stories.

1895. *La Vocation* ('The Vocation'). A novel.

1895. 'Les Tombeaux' ('The Tombs'). A short story.

1896. 'Les Vierges' ('The Virgins'). A short story.

1896. *Les Vies encloses* ('Enclosed Lives'). A collection of poems, incorporating a reprint of *Le Voyage dans les yeux*.

1897. *Le Carillonneur* ('The Carillon-Player'). A novel.

1898. 'L'Arbre' ('The Tree'). A short story.

1898. *Le Miroir du ciel natal* ('The Mirror of the Native Sky').
A collection of free verse poems.

1899. *L'Elite*. A series of essays on writers, orators,
painters and sculptors.

1900. *Le Mirage*. A four-act play adapted by Rodenbach
from *Bruges-la-Morte*, published in the April issue of
Revue de Paris, and as a book in 1901.

1901. *Le Rouet des brumes*. ('The Spinning-Wheel of Mists').
A collection of stories.

1923. *Oeuvres*, Vol. I.

1924. *Evocations*. A selection of articles from newspapers
and magazines between 1883 and 1898.

1925. *Oeuvres*, Vol. II.

A Note on Further Reading

Though interest in the work of Georges Rodenbach has
continued to grow in recent years, there remains little
critical writing on him in English. I would like to suggest
two books to the reader desirous of further knowledge:

Philip Mosley (ed.), *Georges Rodenbach: Critical Essays*.
Madison/Teaneck: Fairleigh Dickinson University Press,
1996.

George C. Schoolfield, *A Baedeker of Decadence: Charting a
Literary Fashion, 1884–1927*. New Haven: Yale University
Press, 2003.

Thus my soul alone, and which nothing influences: it is as if enclosed in glass and in silence, given over entire to its own interior spectacle.

—Georges Rodenbach

Foreword

First and foremost in this study of passion, I have striven to evoke the spirit of a particular city as main character, a city associated with states of mind, one that is able to advise, dissuade, induce action.

In fact, this city of Bruges, which I have chosen with especial pleasure, appears almost human.... It establishes a pervasive influence on its residents, molding them according to its bells and rituals.

What I am seeking to suggest is the city as a guide to action; its urban landscapes are no longer mere back-drops or arbitrary descriptions but are fundamentally involved in the plot of the novel.

The fact that these scenes of Bruges collaborate in the events of the story explains why it matters for me also to have them reproduced visually within the text: quays, deserted streets, old residences, canals, Beguinage, churches, belfries, cult objects. Whoever reads this novel will thus also feel the presence and influence of the city, will experience more vividly the contagiousness of the waters, will themselves become more aware of the tall towers, their shadows lengthening over the text.

G.R.

I

Day was fading, darkening the hallways of the large silent house, fitting crape screens to the window panes.

As was his daily custom in the late afternoon, Hugues Viane was getting ready to go out. Lonely and idle, he tended to spend whole days on the first floor in his vast bedroom, whose windows overlooked the Quai du Rosaire along which, mirrored in the water, stretched the frontage of his house.

He whiled away some of the time by reading magazines and old books, smoked a great deal and, lost in his memories, lingered at the window opening onto the grey weather outside.

For five years now he had lived like this, ever since his arrival in Bruges shortly after the death of his wife. Five years already! And he constantly reminded himself of the fact: 'Widower! To be a widower! I am the widower!' Dull, irremediable word perfectly describing a bereft person.

Separation had proved a terrible experience for him. He had known, after all, an abundance of love. They had traveled together at leisure, the experience of each new country serving to renew their idyllic romance. Not only the untroubled delights of an exemplary married life but also an ever passionate relationship, with its thrilling embraces and its two souls in harmony, detached yet united, like the mingling of parallel quays reflected in a canal.

They had scarcely been aware that ten years of this happiness had passed by so quickly.

Then, just before her thirtieth birthday, the young woman died, after having been confined to her bed for only a few weeks. The sight of her stretched out on her death bed would stay with him forever: grown pale and wasted as if seen by candlelight, she whom he had adored for her beautiful rosy complexion, for her pearl-like eyes with their large black pupils whose darkness contrasted with the amber color of her hair which, when unpinned, flowed long and wavy down her back, like those calm yet quivering tresses seen on the madonnas of the Primitive painters.

Leaning over her dead body, Hugues had cut off this spray of hair, braided during the last days of her illness. Is it not one of death's small mercies that in destroying all, it yet leaves the hair intact? Eyes, lips, all disintegrate but hair even keeps its color. So we survive by hair alone! And now, more than five years later and despite the salt of many tears, the well-preserved tress had barely faded.

On this particular day, the widower was reliving his past all the more painfully on account of the grey weather of November, when the bells scatter the dead ashes of the years, as it were, into the air in a dust of sounds.

Although he had made up his mind in any case to go out, it was not in search of any external distraction or remedy for his suffering. He didn't even consider anything like that. But as evening fell, he liked to wander about, looking for resemblances of his sorrow in the lonely canals and the religious quarters of the city.

Descending to the ground floor, he noticed that some doors which were usually kept closed were standing wide open onto the long white hallway.

In the silence he called for his servant: 'Barbe!... Barbe!...'

The woman, appearing immediately in the first doorway, surmised why her master had summoned her:

'Monsieur, I had to do the drawing rooms today because there is a holiday tomorrow.'

'Which holiday?' asked Hugues, vexed.

'You mean, Monsieur doesn't know? It's the feast of the Presentation of the Blessed Virgin. I have to go to mass and to the evening service at the Beguinage. It's just like Sunday. And since I'll not be working tomorrow, I've tidied the drawing rooms today.'

Hugues Viane was unable to hide his displeasure. Barbe knew full well that he always liked to help her with that particular task. Those two rooms contained too many treasures, too many memories of his wife and of bygone days to let his servant go through them alone. He wanted to be able to supervise her, follow her movements, check on her carefulness, watch for signs of her respect. And when it was necessary to dust some precious bibelot—such as a cushion or fire-screen his wife had made—he wanted to handle it himself. It was as if her fingerprints were still all over this permanently unaltered furniture—sofas, divans, armchairs where she had sat and which preserved, as it were, the imprint of her body. The curtains kept the immortal folds she had given them, while it seemed necessary also to sponge and wipe very carefully the clear surface of the mirrors, so as not to erase her face sleeping deep within them. But Hugues was equally concerned to protect the portraits of his wife, done at different ages and placed here and there, on the mantlepiece, pedestal tables, and walls. Above all— and any accident would have broken his spirit—there was the treasure of the immaculate tress. He hadn't in the least wanted to hide it away in some old chest of drawers or some dark trunk—that would have been like entombing the hair—but preferred, since it was still living and of an ageless gold, to keep it on display rather like the undying aspect of his love.

To be able always to see this tress, which was, to him, still his wife, he had put it on top of the long-silenced piano in the large drawing room which was always kept the same, intending it simply to lie there—a cut tress, a broken chain, a rope saved from a shipwreck. To protect it from contamination, from the damp atmosphere which might have discolored or rusted it, he had this idea—naïve if it hadn't been so touching—of putting it under the transparent cover of a crystal case, so that he could gaze devotedly at the tress every single day.

It seemed to him that this tress was the soul of the house, bound up in the existence of both Hugues and the silent objects living around him.

Barbe, the old Flemish servant, who was a little sullen but devoted and meticulous, knew which precautions were to be taken with regard to these objects, and she herself always approached them in trembling awe. Reticent, in black skirt and tulle bonnet, she resembled a non-resident nun. Moreover, she often went to the Beguinage to see her only relative, Sister Rosalie, who belonged to that order of nuns.

From frequenting the Beguinage, with its pious routines, she had learned the silence and the peculiar gliding step of those accustomed to church floor tiles. And for this reason, that she made no noise or laughter to intrude upon his sorrow, Hugues Viane had found her most suitable ever since his arrival in Bruges. She had been his only servant and had become essential to his existence, in spite of her innocent tyranny, her old maidishness, her devout nature, and her will to do as she pleased, a will very much in evidence on this particular day when, because of a spiritually comforting holiday on the morrow, she had been through the drawing rooms without his knowledge and regardless of his strict orders to the contrary.

Before he went out, Hugues waited for her to rear-range the furniture, assuring himself that everything that was dear to him was intact and put back in the right place. Once his mind was set at rest, he was ready to take his usual twilight stroll, despite the relentless late autumn drizzle, shedding tears, weaving into the water, tacking the air, pricking the still surface of the canals, capturing and paralyzing the soul like a bird trapped in the wet meshes of an endless net.

II

Every day in the late afternoon Hugues followed the same route alongside the quays. Although only forty years old, he already stooped a little and walked uncertainly. His bereavement had brought early autumn to his life, evident in his hair receding at the temples and streaked with grey. His pale eyes had a faraway look, to somewhere beyond life itself.

Bruges was desperately sad on these late afternoons. But Hugues loved it like that. After all, it was for the sake of his own sadness that he had chosen to settle there after his bereavement. He had been there before in happier times on travels with his wife—to Paris, the coast, foreign countries—living as they pleased, a quite cosmopolitan way of life. They had visited Bruges together when its melancholy had not in the least spoiled their sense of delight. Later, alone, he remembered Bruges and had immediately felt an intuitive need to live there. A mysterious equation was forming: the need for a dead city to correspond to his dead wife. His deep mourning demanded an appropriate setting. Only in Bruges would his life remain bearable. So he had gone there instinctively. Let the world elsewhere bustle, hum, get excited over holidays, braid its thousand yarns. He needed unbroken silence, an existence so monotonous as barely allowing him to feel still alive.

Why must silence prevail in the vicinity of physical suffering? Why do we tread so gently in sickrooms? Why do voices and noises seem to cause disturbances and even reopen wounds?

And noise even has a bearing on the suffering of the mind.

In the mute atmosphere of the lifeless waters and streets, Hugues felt his heartache less, and he could think more calmly about his wife. In the line of the canals, he was better able to see and hear her again, to discover her Ophelia face floating along, to listen to her voice in the high-pitched distant song of the carillon.

Equally beautiful and beloved in its former days, the city was the virtual incarnation of Hugues's own loss. Bruges was his wife, while she was Bruges. Their destinies were joined together. This was Bruges-la-Morte, the dead city, entombed in its stone quays, the arteries of its canals chilled to death at the cessation of the great heartbeat of the sea.

As he wandered about on this particular evening, black memories haunted him more than ever, emerging from beneath bridges where faces cry from invisible sources. A sensation of death emanated from the shuttered houses, from windows like eyes blurred in the throes of death, from gables tracing crape staircases in the water. He skirted the Quai Vert, the Quai du Miroir, crossed the Pont du Moulin, disappearing into the sad poplar-fringed suburbs. And everywhere he went, the small salty notes of the parish bells dropped on his head, as if flung from a brush during an absolution.

In the solitude of this autumn evening, the wind sweeping away the last leaves, he felt more than ever a desire to put an end to his life, an impatience for the grave. It seemed as if a shadow from the towers lengthened over his soul; as if the ancient walls offered him their advice; as if a whispering voice rose from the waters which were coming to meet him, as, in the words of Shakespeare's gravediggers, they came to meet Ophelia.

He had already felt thus entrapped. He had heard the slow persuasion of the stones; he had truly surprised 'the order of things' by surviving the death all around him.

For a long time he had seriously considered suicide. Ah, how he had adored that woman whose eyes were still upon him! He still pursued the sound of her voice, fled to the end of the horizon, so far away. What was it about that woman that he remained so totally attached to her, that had deprived him of the rest of the world from the time she had vanished? There must be a kind of love like those Dead Sea fruits that leave an imperishable taste of ashes in the mouth.

It was for her sake only that he had resisted his strong urge to commit suicide. As he reached the dregs of his cup of sorrow, his childhood religious feeling had returned to him. Being of a somewhat mystical temperament, he hoped that nothingness was not the culmination of life, and that one day he would see her again. His religion thus kept him from taking his own life, an act which would have meant banishment from the bosom of God and removal of the vague possibility of seeing her again.

So he kept on living; praying, soothed by thoughts of her awaiting him in some heavenly garden; dreaming of her, in the churches, to the sound of the organ.

He chanced this evening to enter Notre-Dame, where he went often to enjoy the mortuary atmosphere. Everywhere, on the walls, on the ground, were burial slabs with death's heads, their notched names and pitted inscriptions like lips of stone.... Death itself here eaten away by death....

Yet, in close proximity to all this, the nothingness of life was brightened by the consoling vision of a death-enduring love. This was what led Hugues on his frequent pilgrimages to this church—the famous tombs of Charles the Bold and Mary of Burgundy at the far end of a side chapel. Such a stirring sight, especially the gentle Princess Mary lying stiffly on the entablature, palms together, head on a pillow, in a dress of brass feet resting on a dog symbolizing fidelity. Thus was his wife resting forever upon his dark soul, while in time he would, like the Duke, repose beside her. If they were not to be reunited in the Christian life hereafter, they would at least sleep side by side in the welcome refuge of death.

Hugues's normal dinner time was fast approaching. Feeling sadder than ever, he left Notre-Dame and made his way towards home. He sought the memory of his wife in order to apply it to the form and size of the tomb he had been contemplating and to imagine all of this with another face. But the expression of the dead, held in our memories for a while, first starts to fade, then slowly wastes away, like the dust disappearing from an unglassed pastel. So, deep within us, the dead then die a second time.

Suddenly, looking deeply into his inner self, Hugues made a firm effort to recompose his already nearly eroded features. Ordinarily, he barely noticed the passers-by, scarce as they were, but now he felt a sudden excitement on seeing a young woman come towards him from the other end of the street. At first he hadn't noticed her at all, approaching from the other end of the street; it was only when she came close by him.

Seeing her, he stopped short, as if frozen to the spot. An apparition, surely, this person who had just passed him by. Hugues's eyes seemed to roll for a minute; he put his hand over them as if warding off a dream. Then, after a moment's hesitation, he turned towards the stranger who was moving away with a slow, rhythmic walk. Retreating, he left the quay he had been on and began to follow her. Shifting quickly from one sidewalk to the other, he caught up with her, and watched her with an insistence which would have been improper had she not seemed totally entranced. Unconcerned, seeing but not looking, the young woman continued on her way while Hugues looked increasingly strange and haggard. He had been following her now for several minutes from street to street, sometimes closing in on her as if to discover her exact identity, then dropping back in apparent fright when it seemed he was becoming too forward. He seemed drawn and terrified at the same time, as by the depth of a well in which one seeks to make out a face....

Yes! This time he recognized her! That pastel complexion, those large dark pupils in pearl-like eyes, they were the same. And while he walked behind her, that hair which appeared over the nape of her neck under her black bonnet and veil was clearly the same golden color, really a silky amber, a fluid textured yellow. The same contrast between nocturnal eyes and blazing noon of hair.

Was he on the verge of losing his mind? Or else his retina, having preserved the image of his wife for so long, identified her in the passers-by. Here was this woman appearing suddenly out of nowhere to offer him the face he constantly sought. Her face was simply too identical, too much of a twin. Such a vision was so perturbing, a miracle almost terrifyingly close to a total identity.

And everything—her walk, her size, the rhythm of her body, the expression of her features, that inward look which was no longer only line and color, but also spirituality of being and movement of soul—everything had returned, had reappeared, was alive!

Mechanically now, like a somnambulist, not even asking himself why, Hugues kept following her through the misty maze of the streets of Bruges. Reaching a crossroads, with its confusion of directions, he lost sight of her all of a sudden. He had been some way behind her and now she had vanished down he knew not which one of those winding sidestreets.

He stopped, peering into the distance, scanning the empty scene in front of him, tears welling up in his eyes....

How like his dead wife she was!

III

This encounter troubled Hugues greatly. When he dreamed of his wife, he now saw only this stranger from the other evening; she was a perfect living memory, exact in every respect, stronger in his mind than his wife herself.

When he went in silent devotion to kiss the relic of preserved hair or found himself moved to tears before one or another of her portraits, he no longer confronted the image of the dead woman but rather that of the living person who resembled her. The mysterious identification of those two faces was as if fate smiled upon him, offering him landmarks for his memory, conniving with him against forgetfulness, substituting a fresh imprint for an already yellowed and fading one ravaged by time.

Hugues now possessed a distinctly new vision of his vanished wife. All he had to do was call to mind the old quay the other day in the falling dark and a woman with his wife's face approaching him. He no longer needed to look far behind him through the perspective of the years; it was enough to dream of the evening before or the one before that. Everything now was plain and simple. His eyes had stored up anew that dearly loved face; the recent impression had fused with the old, each fortifying the other, in a resemblance that now was giving almost the illusion of a real presence.

During the next few days, Hugues grew completely obsessed by the existence of a woman who was identical to his lost wife. Having watched the woman pass by, he had for a minute a cruel dream that his wife was going to return, had returned, and was approaching him as in the past. The same eyes, same hair, same complexion—all alike and sufficient. Strange twist of nature and of fate!

He would have liked to see her again but perhaps he would never do so. However, just to know she was somewhere nearby and to be able to meet her made him feel much less lonely and bereft. Is a man still truly a widower, whose wife is only absent and occasionally reappears?

He imagined rediscovering his wife when next he met the woman who resembled her. In hope of this, he went at the same time in the evening to the parts of the city where he had seen her. He strode along the old quay with its darkened gables where bored women, suddenly interested in his movements, watched him from behind windows muffled with muslin curtains; he plunged down dead streets and tortuous alleyways, hoping to see her suddenly emerge at some crossroads or around some corner.

A week passed thus, with nothing but disappointment. Hugues was already letting his hope of seeing her slip from his mind when, one Monday—the same day as the first meeting—he saw her again, recognizing her immediately as she approached him with the same poised walk. Even more than on the previous occasion, she appeared to him as a total resemblance, absolute and truly frightening.

In his excitement, his heart had almost stopped beating; he felt as if he would die. Blood rang in his ears while his eyes grew blurred with visions of white muslin, wedding veils and processions of communicants. Then, all black and close, her shadow like a stain was about to darken him.

This time the woman had undoubtedly noticed his agitated state since she looked at him with an air of surprise. That look, coming from nothingness, belonged to him again; that look he had never believed he would see again—imagining it diluted into the earth—was now upon him, soft and steady, reviving and caressing him; that look from afar, risen from the tomb, like the look that Lazarus must have had for Christ.

Hugues felt totally spent, his whole being swept along in the wake of this vision. There she was in front of him, his lost love, walking up to him, then walking away. He felt impelled to follow her footsteps, approach her, look at her, drink in her rediscovered eyes, light up his life again in the glow of her hair. He would unquestionably have to follow her to the end of the city and to the end of the world.

Not even considering it rationally, he walked behind her again, this time keeping close, breathless with fear of losing her a second time across this old city of meandering, circuitous streets.

Following a woman! He hadn't for one minute dreamed of such abnormal behaviour on his part. But this was different: the woman he was following, was accompanying on this twilight walk, the woman he would lead back to her tomb, was *his* wife....

Totally magnetized, Hugues kept walking as if in a dream alongside or just behind the stranger, not even noticing that they had left the deserted quays for the commercial heart of the city, the Grand'Place where, vast and dark, the Tour des Halles shielded itself from the invading night with the gold buckler of its dark clockface.

Seemingly trying to shake off her pursuer, the lithe and swift young woman took the Rue Flamande—with its old sculpted, ornate facades like ships' decks—where she reappeared in a silhouette more clearly outlined each time she passed in front of a lighted shop window or beneath the broad halo of a street lamp.

Then he saw her cross the road abruptly, make her way towards the open doors of the theater and go in.

This didn't stop Hugues.... He had become an inert will, a trailing satellite. The movement of the soul gathers its own momentum. Obeying the earlier impulse, he pressed his way into the foyer where the crowd was thronging. But the vision had vanished. The young woman was nowhere to be perceived, not among the members of the public lining up for tickets, not at the entrance to the auditorium, not on the staircases. Where had she disappeared to? Down which corridor? Through which side door? He had seen her go in, there was no doubt about that. Surely she was going to see the show. Then she would shortly be in the auditorium. Perhaps she was already seated comfortably, perhaps in the plush obscurity of a box. He had to find her, see her again, contemplate her throughout an evening! He felt his head spinning at this thought, one that gave him a sense of well being and pain at the same time. He wouldn't have dreamed of resisting the idea. He didn't stop to reflect on the disordered attractions to which he had abandoned himself for the last hour, or on the craziness of his latest project, or on the anomaly of his presence at a theatrical performance in spite of the great sorrow with which he was eternally cloaked. He made his way without hesitation to the box office, paid for a seat, and went in.

His eyes quickly scoured every seat in the house, the orchestra rows, the boxes on each level, the balconies that were slowly filling up, illuminated by the contagious gleam of the chandeliers. Unable to find her, he felt sad, anxious and disconcerted. What kind of evil trick was being played on him? The vision of a face at first revealed, then concealed from him? Intermittent visions like the moon through clouds! He waited, looked round again. Some latecomers hurried in, finding their seats in a squeaking of doors and benches.

Only she did not arrive.

He began to regret his rash action, all the more since he could sense that people were astonished to notice his presence through their opera-glasses. It was true, he mixed with no one, had no contact with any family, lived alone. But he was well known locally, by sight at least. People knew who he was and all about his noble despair. This was Bruges, after all, that sparsely populated and lethargic city where everyone knew everyone else, made inquiries concerning any newcomers, and kept their neighbours informed about them.

It was a surprise, almost the end of a legend; and the triumph of those malicious persons to whose faces the mention of the inconsolable widower had always brought knowing smiles.

By who knows what influence that flows from a crowd unified in a common thought, Hugues became aware of a personal error of judgement, of a perjured dignity, of a first crack in the vase of his conjugal cult, from which his sorrow, well contained until now, would totally drain away.

The orchestra, however, had just begun the overture to the opera being performed whose title, *Robert le Diable,* was printed in capitals on his neighbor's program. It was one of those old-fashioned operas on which provincial repertoires are almost invariably based. Now the violins were unfolding the first bars.

Hugues felt even more troubled. Since the death of his wife, he had listened to no music at all, fearing the sound of musical instruments. Even a street accordion with its asthmatic and slightly sour wheeze could bring him to tears, as could the organs on a

Sunday at Notre-Dame and Sainte-Walburge when
they seemed to drape the assembled faithful with
black velvet and catafalques of sound.

Now the opera music was drowning his brain; the
bowing of the violins was playing on his nerves. His
eyes smarted: was he about to dissolve in tears again?
As he contemplated leaving, a strange thought
crossed his mind: he was certain that the woman
he sought—as if in a fit of madness and desire for the
balm of her resemblance—was not there, although he
had followed her inside the theater almost beneath
her eyes. But if she were not to be found anywhere in
the auditorium, might she perhaps be about to
appear on stage?

Even to speculate on such a profanation tore at his
soul. The same face, that of his wife herself, revealed
by the footlights, underlined by make-up. What if the
woman he had followed up to her abrupt disappear-
ance through a service door were an actress and he
were about to see her appear before him, singing and
gesturing? Would her voice continue the diabolical
resemblance, that voice—low-pitched yet metallic like
silver mixed with a little bronze—which he had never
again heard, never?

Hugues was stunned by the possibility of pursuing
this chance encounter right to the end; he waited full
of anguish with a kind of premonition that his suspicions would prove to be correct.

Scene gave way to scene but he was none the wiser.
He didn't recognize her among the singers nor in the
chorus, rouged and painted like a row of wooden
dolls. In any case, he was uninterested in the opera
and had resolved to leave after the nuns' scene, whose
graveyard setting was now drawing him back into
his most morbid thoughts. But all of a sudden, during the scene-setting recitative, when the ballerinas,

representing the sisters of the convent awakened from the dead, move in a long line, and Helena, rejecting shroud and gown, comes to life on her tomb, Hugues felt disturbed, like a man emerging from a dark dream and entering a festive room whose light flickers in the toppling scales of his eyes.

It was her—a dancer! But not for one minute did he dream that this was what she was. She was his wife, descending from the stone of her sepulcher, *his* wife who was now smiling, advancing, holding out her arms.

So close a resemblance brought Hugues to the point of tears, with her eyes whose bistre accentuated the surrounding dimness, with the unique tone of that golden hair....

The curtain soon fell on this startlingly fleeting vision.

Stunned yet beaming, head on fire, Hugues returned along the quays, as if still entranced by the persistent vision in his mind's eye, his frame of light even in the dark of night.... Just like Faust hounded by the magic mirror that revealed the heavenly image of woman!

IV

Hugues wasted no time in finding out about her. With star billing on the poster, her name was Jane Scott. She lived in Lille and came with her company twice a week to perform in Bruges.

Dancers are rarely mistaken for prudes. So one evening, induced to get closer to her by the sorrowful charm of that resemblance, he accosted her.

As if expecting this encounter, she replied in an unsurprised voice, the sound of which struck Hugues to the soul. The voice, too, his wife's voice, fully the same and heard once more, wrought in identical silver. The demon of analogy was playing with him! Unless, of course, there is a secret harmony in faces or a match between certain voices, certain pairs of eyes, certain heads of hair.

Since she had, in addition to the rare golden hair of matchless alloy, his wife's dark dilated pearl-like eyes, why wouldn't she also have her speech? Seeing her now more closely, from very close up, he could ascertain no difference between this woman and his wife. Hugues remained confounded by this, and by the fact that this woman—powdered, rouged, burned by the footlights—could still have that same natural, unblemished flesh. Nor was the vulgar style of dancers anywhere evident in her bearing; she dressed soberly, seemed quite gentle and reserved.

Hugues saw her again, chatted to her on several occasions. The spell of the resemblance was working on him.... Yet he had no thought of returning to the theater. Fate had pulled the strings delightfully on that first evening. Since she represented the illusion of his rediscovered wife, it was right that she had seemed to him at first like someone risen from the dead, coming down from a tomb amidst fairy tale moonlit scenery.

From now on he intended to imagine her differently—as his wife made woman again, recommencing her life in the shadows, dressing once more in soft clothes. In order to keep the evocation intact, Hugues wanted the dancer to dress accordingly, so that the two women would resemble each other exactly.

He visited her frequently now on her every trip to the city, waiting at the hotel where she stayed. At first he was happy with the consoling lie of her face, as he sought in it his wife's own expression. He would gaze at her for minutes on end with a sorrowful joy, taking full stock of her lips, her hair, her coloring, tracing them with the flow of his weary eyes.... He felt a surge of ecstatic joy as if a deep well presumed to be empty now yielded a presence. The water is no longer naked; the mirror lives.

To create a further illusion, he often lowered his eyelids while listening to her, drinking in that almost unmistakable voice. The only difference was an occasional lowering in tone, a little wadding around her words that made them sound like his wife speaking from behind a thick curtain.

However, an upsetting memory remained of that first appearance on stage, when he had caught sight of her bare arms, bare throat and supple line of her back. He now began to imagine this body in the stored-away dresses that had belonged to his wife.

A sensual curiosity crept over him.

Who can describe the passionate embraces of two lovers separated for a long time? In this case, death had only been an absence since the same woman had come back again.

Looking at Jane, Hugues thought about his wife, their embraces, their kisses. By possessing this woman, he would be able to repossess the other. What had seemed finished for ever was about to start all over again. And he would not even be cheating his wife, since he would still be loving her in this effigy, and would be kissing that mouth just like hers.

Hugues thus knew both dismal and violent joys. He felt his passion to be good and not sacrilegious, such was the fusion of these two women—lost, found, always loved, in the present as in the past, blessed with identical eyes, hair, skin and body—into a single being to whom he would remain faithful.

Each time now that Jane came to Bruges, Hugues met up with her, whether late afternoon before the performance or afterwards, especially in the silent midnights when, until very late, he remained enraptured by her. Even though his great grief was intact, even though her hotel room had a strange and transient atmosphere, he succeeded gradually in convincing himself that the bad times had never been, that he had never known anything but a loving home, his first and only wife, the quiet intimacy of married life.

The tranquil evenings: private room, interior peace, the unity of the self-sufficient couple, silence and quietist peace! The eyes, like moths, have forgotten everything: the dark corners, the cold window panes, the rain outside, the winter, the carillons sounding the death of the hours—eyes which now flitted only in the narrow ring of lamplight.

Hugues relived those nights.... Total forgetfulness! New beginnings! Time flows down a slope, on a bed without stones.... And it seems that, living, we are already in eternity.

V

Hugues installed Jane in a pleasant house he rented for her along a promenade which ended in suburbs of greenery and windmills.

At the same time, he had persuaded her to leave the theater, to be always beside him in Bruges. He hadn't given a moment's thought to the absurdity of a man of his age and seriousness, well known for his inconsolable and notorious grief, falling madly in love with a dancer. To tell the truth, he didn't love her. All he wanted to be able to do was immortalize the allure of this mirage. When he took her head in his hands and brought it close to him, it was to look into her eyes, searching them for something he had seen in others: a nuance, a reflection, pearls, even some flowers with roots in the soul—and which perhaps were also floating there.

On other occasions, he would untie her hair and let it inundate her shoulders, matching it mentally to an absent tress as if he would spin them together.

Jane didn't pretend to understand Hugues's peculiar behavior or his silent raptures.

She recalled his inexplicable sadness when she had told him, at the beginning of their relationship, that she dyed her hair. Ever since then he had watched with great emotion to see whether she was keeping its shade the same.

'I don't want to dye it any more,' she said one day.

He had seemed highly disturbed by this, insisting that she keep it that clear gold he loved so much. And, while saying that, he had caressed it, running his fingers through it, like a miser rediscovering his treasure.

He also mumbled confusingly: 'Don't change anything.... I love you because you're like this! You don't know, you'll never know what I feel in your hair....'

He seemed to want to say more but stopped, as if on the edge of an abyss of confidences.

Since she had been installed in Bruges, he visited her almost every day, generally spending his evenings at her home, and occasionally dining with her, even though the following day his old servant Barbe would grumble about having unnecessarily cooked and waited for him. Barbe pretended to believe that he had really eaten in a restaurant but, deep down, remained incredulous, finding it hard to recognize her previously so punctual and home-loving master.

Hugues went out a great deal, dividing his time between his own and Jane's house.

He preferred to go there towards evening; this was largely a matter of habit but also to avoid undue notice on his way to the house he had deliberately chosen in an isolated area. He felt no shame or embarrassment because he knew that the motives and the stratagems of this transposition were not only an excuse, but also absolution and rehabilitation before his wife and almost before God. But he still had to reckon with the prudishness of the province. How could he possibly not worry a little about the neighbors, about public hostility and respect, when he felt people's eyes were incessantly upon him, as if touching him?

All this was particularly true in this strict Catholic city, this Bruges with its tall stone-cowled towers casting their shadows over all, while a contempt for the secret roses of the flesh seemed to emanate from the convent houses. Here was a contagious glorification of chastity. Madonnas on every street corner in cases of wood and glass. Dressed in velvet coats and set among artificial flowers, they held out the unrolled text of a banderole that, on its side, proclaimed, 'I am the Immaculate One.'

In Bruges, passion and extramarital relations are always perverse acts, paths to hell, the sin of the Sixth and Ninth Commandments that brings the color of confusion to the faces of penitents and causes them to speak in hushed tones in the confessionals.

Knowing about this austerity of Bruges, Hugues had avoided offending it. But nothing escapes attention in such a meager provincial life. Unbeknown to him, he was arousing pious indignation at his behavior. Scandalized faith willingly expresses itself in ironic jibes. Thus, the cathedral laughed and flouted the devil with the masks of its gargoyles.

When the affair between widower and dancer was talked about, he unwittingly became the laughing stock of the town. Everyone knew about it: gossip and scandal spread from door to door; idle talk, hearkened to with beguine-like inquisitiveness; weeds of scandalmongering that, in the dead cities, push up between all the cobblestones.

Everyone enjoyed themselves more with the history of his long despair, his unrelieved sorrow, all his thoughts singly gathered and bunched in a bouquet for a grave. Today, the sorrow that everyone had believed eternal had come to an end.

Everyone had been fooled by it, even the poor widower himself, who undoubtedly had been bewitched by a hussy. She was well known. She was a former theater dancer. They let her know it, too, as she went around town, while laughing, while growing a little indignant at her air of calmness that, they found, was totally betrayed by her dancing walk and blonde hair. They even knew where she lived and that the widower went to see her every evening. A little more, and they would have told the times and routes....

On long drawn out afternoons, the inquisitive townsfolk would watch him go by. They sat at casement windows, spying on him with the aid of small mirrors known as *espions,* attached to the outer window ledge of almost every house. These oblique mirrors frame the equivocal profiles of the street: little reflecting traps that, unbeknown to passers-by, capture all their antics, their smiles and gestures, a minute's thoughtful look in their eyes—transmitting all of it to the interiors of houses where someone is keeping watch.

Thus, thanks to this betrayal by mirror, Hugues's comings and goings were quickly common knowledge, as was each detail of the semi-concubinage in which he was now living with Jane. The illusion in which he persisted, his naive precautions of going to see her only at dusk, grafted a kind of absurdity onto the relationship which at first had offended, and the indignation ended in laughter.

Hugues suspected nothing. And he continued to go out as darkness fell, making his way to the adjacent suburb by determined detours.

How less painful these twilight walks were for him now! He crossed the city, the hundred-year-old bridges, the deathly quays along which the water sighs. The evening bells rang for some memorial service the following day. Oh! the full peal of those bells, but, it seemed, drifting away and already so far from him, tolling as if in other skies....

That the rain spouts dripped, that the tunnel below the bridge wept cold tears, that the waterside poplars rustled like the lament of a frail and inconsolable spring, all were in vain. For Hugues no longer heard this sorrow of things, nor saw the hard edges of the city as if swaddled in the thousand bandages of its canals.

The city of the past, this Bruges-la-Morte, whose widower also he seemed to be, only touched him now with a glaze of melancholy. Consoled, he walked on, through its silence, as if Bruges too had broken out of its tomb and was offering itself as a new city resembling the old.

While he went each evening to find Jane again, he felt not a stroke of remorse; nor, for one minute, any feeling of perjury, of the great love sunk into parody, of the abandoned sorrow—not even that small shiver that runs through the widow's marrow when she fastens a red rose to her crape and cashmere.

VI

Hugues thought: What indefinable power there is in resemblance!

It corresponds to two contradictory needs in human nature: habit and novelty. That law of habit was the very rhythm of being. Hugues had experienced it so acutely that he felt it alone would decide his fate. Having lived with so dear a woman for ten years, he could not put her out of his mind, continuing to concern himself with her and searching for her face in the faces of others.

On the other hand, the taste for novelty is no less instinctive. One grows tired of possessing the same good things. As with health, one only enjoys it in the awareness of its opposite. Love also needs its periods of respite and change.

It is precisely resemblance that reconciles habit and novelty, balancing them out, fusing them at some indefinite point, acting as their horizon line.

Principally, in the case of love, this kind of refinement works in the charm of a new woman resembling the old!

Hugues, whom sorrow and solitude had for so long made sensitive to such nuances of the soul, enjoyed this charm with increasing delight and ecstasy. Furthermore, wasn't it some innate sense of desirable analogies that had brought him to Bruges in the first place?

He possessed an extra sense, what might be called 'the sense of resemblance,' fragile and subtle, connecting things by a thousand tenuous strands, relating even the trees by the threads of the Holy Virgin, creating an intangible telegraphy between his soul and the inconsolable towers.

That is why he had chosen Bruges, that city from which the sea—like a great happiness also—had retreated.

The unison of his mind and this greatest of grey cities was in itself an example of this phenomenon of resemblance.

Melancholy of these grey streets of Bruges, where every day seemed like All Saints Day! This greyness, as if made with white convent coifs and black priestly cassocks, whose passage here was incessant and contagious. Mystery of this greyness, of an eternal feeling of grief.

Along every street, the facades seem to shade into infinity: some of a pale green wash or showing the faded brick repointed in white; but, others, very close by, dark and austere charcoal drawings, burned etchings whose inks set off rather brighter adjacent ones; and overall, the same greyness that emanates, floating and propagating itself along the line of walls ranged like miniature quays.

The sound of the bells also comes over as rather black; now, muffled and melting in the air, it turns to an equally grey clamor drifting along, glancing off and undulating on the water of the canals.

And this water itself, in spite of so many reflections—corners of blue sky, roof tiles, snowy swans sailing by, green waterside poplars—unifies itself in colorless paths of silence.

By a climatic miracle, a mutual penetration, an unexpected atmospheric chemistry, the brightest colors are neutralized, reduced to a single dream, an amalgam of rather grey drowsiness.

It is as if the frequent mist, the veiled northern light, the granite quays, the incessant rain and the pervasive peal of bells had influenced by their alliance the very color of the air—and also, in this ancient city, the dead embers of time, the steady silent accumulation of grains in the hour-glass of the years.

That is why Hugues had wanted to retire there, so that he would surely feel his last drops of energy imperceptibly drying up, sinking beneath this fine eternal dust, also making his soul grey, the color of the city.

Today, by a sudden seemingly miraculous encounter, this sense of resemblance had acted again, but this time inversely. How and by what quirk of fate had that face brusquely surged into view to revive all his early memories in this Bruges so distant from them?

Although it was an extraordinary chance, Hugues abandoned himself henceforth to the intoxication of this resemblance between Jane and the dead woman, as formerly he had exulted in the resemblance between himself and the city.

VII

Over the few months since Hugues had met Jane, nothing had affected his lie of reliving the past.

How his life had changed! He wasn't sad any more. He no longer had that impression of solitude in an enormous void. Jane had brought back to him his former love that had seemed so far away and out of reach. He was rediscovering his wife and seeing her quite the same as the moon is seen reflected in a pool of water. So far no cruel wind had brought the slightest wrinkle, nor any shiver to distort the fullness of her reflection.

And it was so clearly the dead woman whom he continued to honor by the simulacrum of this resemblance, which he had never for one moment believed to lack fidelity to his cult or memory of her. Each morning, since the day after her death, he had devoted himself—as at the stations on the way of love's cross—to his mementos of her. Immediately on rising, he would go deliberately to linger in front of his wife's portraits in the silent shadow of the drawing-rooms with their half-opened blinds and always undisturbed furniture. Here a photograph of her as a young woman a little before they were engaged; here, in the middle of a panel, a large pastel whose reflecting frame first revealed her, then hid her again, in an intermittent silhouette; there, on a pedestal table, another photograph in an enamel inlaid frame, a portrait from the later years when like a drooping lily she already wore an air of suffering.... Hugues placed his lips on them, and kissed them as if they were patens or reliquaries.

Each morning he would also contemplate the crystal casket where his wife's hair, always visible, rested. But there was no rest for it if he kept on lifting the lid. He wouldn't have dared pick it up, nor entwine it around his fingers. That hair was sacred! It was the very piece of the dead woman that had escaped the tomb to sleep a better sleep in this glass coffin. But it was dead all the same, it came from a death, and was never to be touched. He had to be satisfied with just looking at it, reassuring himself that it remained intact, that it was always present, this hair upon which depended, perhaps, the very life of the house.

Hugues thus passed long hours reviving his memories while above his head, in the enclosed silence of the rooms, the chandelier gave out from its aspergillum of shivering crystal a gentle spluttering sigh.

And then he went to Jane's house as at his final devotional station, Jane who possessed the full living head of hair, Jane who was like the portrait most resembling the dead woman. One day, even, trying to deceive himself over a more particular identification, Hugues was immediately seduced by a strange idea. He didn't wish only to preserve his wife's baubles, sundry objects or portraits but to keep everything of hers as if she were only absent. Nothing had been misappropriated, given away or sold. Her bedroom was kept always ready as if for her possible return, neat and tidy, exactly as before, with fresh springs of boxwood blessed annually. Her linen from former days was entirely stacked in drawers full of sachets which kept it intact in its slightly yellowed immobility. The dresses, too, all the old clothes hung in the armoires, silks and poplins, emptied of motion.

Hugues wished to see them again occasionally, keen to forget nothing, to eternalize his sorrow....

Love, like faith, is kept up by little observances. One day, a strange desire crossed his mind that instantly haunted him until its realization: to see Jane in one of those gowns, dressed like the dead woman, whom she already so resembled, adding to the facial identity that of one of the outfits, which he had formerly seen adapted to someone of identical size. It would be even more so the return of his wife.

What a divine moment, when Jane would approach him thus attired, a moment that would abolish both time and reality, that would give him total forgetfulness!

Once it entered into his mind, this idea became a fixation, obsessive....

One morning, he finally decided: to call his old servant and instruct her to bring down from the attic a trunk which would serve to carry a few of these precious dresses.

'Is Monsieur going on a journey?' asked old Barbe who, unable to explain to herself the new way of life of her formerly so recluse master, his absences, his meals out, and his departures, began to assume that he was going crazy.

He got her to help him unhook the dresses, sort through them and shake off the dust which rose in clouds in the neglected armoires.

He chose two dresses, the last two his wife had bought, and laid them out carefully in the trunk, flattening the skirts and smoothing out the creases.

Barbe understood nothing of this, but it shocked her to see this hitherto untouched wardrobe being separated. Wondering whether it was to be sold, she ventured to say:

'What would poor Madame say?'

Hugues looked at her. He had turned pale. Had she guessed? Did she know?

'What do you mean by that?' he demanded.

'I think,' replied old Barbe, 'that in my village in Flanders, if a dead person's clothes are not sold immediately, during the week after burial, they must be kept the rest of one's life, on pain of keeping the departed one in Purgatory until one's own death.'

'Be calm,' said Hugues, relieved. 'I have no intention of selling anything. Your folklore is right.'

A short while later Barbe was thus astounded when, despite what he had just said, she saw the trunk being loaded onto a fiacre and him leave with it.

Hugues didn't know how to put his crazy idea to Jane, for out of a kind of delicacy, of modesty with regard to his wife, he had never spoken to her about his past, nor even alluded to the sweet and cruel resemblance that he traced in her.

The trunk set before her, Jane let out little cries of pleasure, jumping about: What a surprise! He had doubtless filled it to overflowing. What? Gifts? A dress?

'Yes, dresses,' said Hugues mechanically.

'Oh! You are so kind! Then there's more than one?'

'Two.'

'What color? Quick, let me see!'

And she drew close to him, holding out her hand, asking for the key.

Hugues didn't know what to say. He dared not speak, not wanting to betray himself, to explain the morbid desire to which he had impulsively succumbed.

Once the trunk was opened, Jane disinterred the dresses from the trunk and took them in with a quick glance, evidently disappointed.

'What an ugly style! And this design in silk, how old it is, old! But where did you buy such dresses? And the cloth of this skirt! It's been out of fashion for ten years. I believe you're trying to make a fool of me!'

Hugues remained perplexed and very shamefaced; he searched for words, an explanation, not the true one, but one that would serve. He began to see the absurdity of his idea, although its fascination still gripped him.

If only she would agree! If only she would put on one of the dresses just for a minute!—and this minute would truly contain for him all the paroxysm of resemblance and the infinity of forgetfulness.

His cajoling voice explained to her: Yes, they were old dresses... that he'd inherited... a relative's dresses... he had wanted to joke... had wanted to see her in one of them. It was crazy; but he had wanted it... just for a minute!...

Jane understood nothing of this; laughed, turned each garment over and over, this way and that, feeling the barely faded rich silk but remaining astounded by the strange and faintly ridiculous style which nonetheless had once been both elegant and fashionable....

Hugues insisted.

'But you'll find me ugly!'

At first bewildered by this caprice, Jane finally treated dressing up in these cast-offs as a great joke. Laughing girlishly, she took off her peignoir and, bare-armed, adjusting the bodice which covered her corset, put on a low-cut dress.... Standing in front of the mirror, Jane laughed to see herself thus: 'I look like an old portrait!'

And she smirked, twisted and turned; climbed onto the table, hitching up her skirts, to see herself full length, still laughing, her throat shaking, one end of her chemise badly done up and showing the bodice beneath, revealing her bare skin, less than chaste, and evidence of the intimacies of lingerie....

Hugues reflected. This minute, which had been his dream of supreme culmination, seemed trivial and cheapened. Jane was enjoying the game. Overcome by wild hilarity, she now wanted to try on the other dress and started to dance a set of choreographed steps.

Hugues felt a growing anguish of spirit; he had the impression of taking part in a sorrowful masquerade. For the first time, the fascination of physical conformity could not suffice. It had still worked but perversely. Without the resemblance, Jane struck him as only vulgar. Because of the resemblance, she gave him momentarily that atrocious impression of seeing the dead woman again, but degraded in spite of the identical face and dress—the impression that one experiences on holy days in the evening, when one chances to meet impersonators of the Virgin Mary or the Holy Sisters still costumed in coats and pious tunics but a little tipsy, caught up in a mystical carnival under the street lamps whose wounds bleed into the darkness.

VIII

One Easter Sunday in March, old Barbe learned from her master in the morning that he would not be having dinner or supper at home and that she was free until the evening. This news delighted her, for since her day off coincided with a great holiday, she would go to the Beguinage and participate in all the services: high mass, evensong and the benedictory service. She would spend the rest of the day with her relative, Sister Rosalie, who lived in one of the principal convents of the religious enclosure.

To go to the Beguinage was one of the best, one of the few of Barbe's joys. Everyone there knew her. She was friendly with several of the beguines and dreamed of her very old age when, having amassed some savings, she would herself come there, don the veil and end her life like so many others—so happy!—whom she saw with a cornet swathing their aged heads of ivory.

Especially on this adolescent March morning, she exulted in heading for her dear Beguinage, with a still sprightly step, her large black hooded cloak swaying like a bell. In the distance, the unanimous peal of the parish bells seemed to harmonize with her walk. Among them, every quarter hour, the tremulous high-pitched music of the carillon, a tune as if strummed on a glass piano....

Some early spring grass gave a rural air to the suburb. Although Barbe had been in service in the city for more than thirty years, she had kept, like her peers, the persistent memory of her village, a peasant soul touched by a little leafiness or a stretch of grass.

The fine morning! And how she went briskly in the bright sunshine, moved by the cry of a bird, by the smell of young shoots in this already rustic suburb with its verdant, chosen setting for the Minnewater— the Lake of Love, as it has been translated, but even better: the water where one loves! And there, in front of this drowsy mere, the lilies like the hearts of first communicants, the turfed slopes full of flowerets, the great trees, the gesticulating windmills on the horizon, Barbe again had the illusion of journeying, of returning, across fields, towards her childhood days....

She was also possessed of a pious spirit, of that Flemish faith in which a little of Spanish Catholicism still exists, that faith in which scruples and terror prevail over trust, and the fear of hell is greater than the dream of heaven. Along with, however, a love of decoration, of the sensuality of flowers, of incense, of rich fabrics, a love which belongs uniquely to the race. This is why the dark soul of the old servant was ecstatic in anticipation of the ceremonies of the holy services, as she was crossing the arched bridge of the Beguinage and entering within the mystical walls.

Here, already, a church-like silence; even the noise of tiny springs running into the lake outside came over like a sound of praying mouths; and the low walls all around, marking out the various convents, white like communion table cloths. In the middle, a meadow straight out of Jan van Eyck, with neat, rich grass and a grazing sheep reminiscent of the paschal lamb.

Streets, named after saints or the blessed, turn and run off at angles, interlace, stretch out, creating a medieval hamlet: a small, separate and more deathly city within the other city. So empty, so contagiously silent, that one walks and speaks softly there, as in the vicinity of a sick person.

If some passer-by chances to approach and makes a noise, one has the impression of something abnormal and sacrilegious. The deadened atmosphere of the place is really only for a few beguines who walk there with light steps, for they seem to glide rather than walk; if anything they are swans, sisters of the white swans of the long canals. When Barbe headed for the church, whence came already the echo of the organ and the singing of the mass, some of these nuns who had been delayed were hurrying beneath the elm bank. She entered the church with the beguines who, lining up near the choir, took their places in the double row of sculpted wooden pews. All the coifs came together, their starched linen wings white with traced reflections of red and blue as the sun shone through the stained glass windows. Barbe watched enviously from a distance, hoping one day herself to become one of this kneeling group of sisters of the community, brides of Jesus and servants of God.

She had taken her place in one of the side aisles of the church, among a few other zealous lay persons: old men, children, poor families lodging in the growing number of empty houses in the Beguinage. Barbe, who couldn't read, was telling a large rosary, her lips praying urgently, looking over occasionally to the side where her relative, Sister Rosalie, was second in place in the pews after the Reverend Mother.

How beautiful the church was, all brazened with lighted candles. Barbe went during the offertory to buy a small candle from the vestry nun, who stood by a wrought iron frame where soon the old servant's offering was burning in turn.

From time to time she followed the burning down of her candle, which she recognized amidst the others.

How happy she was! And how right the priests are to say the church is the House of God! Especially since in the Beguinage it was the sisters who sang in the organ-loft, with soft voices which could only have been those of the angels.

Barbe never wearied of listening to the harmonium, to the canticles which unfolded quite white like beautiful linen.

Meanwhile, mass was said; the lights were going out.

All together, in a shuddering of their cornets, the beguines made their way out—a swarm that took off and strewed the green garden momentarily with a white span, with a flight of gulls. Barbe followed her relative Rosalie at a respectably discreet distance; then, on seeing Rosalie go back into her convent, Barbe quickened her pace and, a moment later, entered too.

There are a number of beguines in each of the residences which constitute the community. Three or four here, fifteen or twenty there. Sister Rosalie's convent was one of the fuller ones; as Barbe walked into the great work room, all the sisters, only just back from church, were laughing, chatting and questioning one another. On account of the holiday, the baskets full of needlework and the squares of lace were laid out in the corners. Some of the nuns were out in the small garden in front of their home, inspecting the plants, the growth of the box-lined flower-beds. Others, some quite young, were showing off the sugar-coated Easter eggs they had received as presents. Somewhat intimidated, Barbe followed her relative in and out of the bedrooms and common rooms packed with visitors, afraid to be alone, to seem intrusive, waiting a little anxiously for the customary invitation to dinner. But then something else! What if today there were too many visiting relatives for her to get a place at table?

Barbe was reassured when Sister Rosalie came to invite her on behalf of the Reverend Mother, apologizing for having left her on her own, bustling about, for

it was her turn among the beguines to run the household for a week.

'We'll chat after dinner,' she added, 'especially since
I've something very serious to tell you.'

'Serious?' asked Barbe, scared. 'Then tell me right
now.'

'I haven't time.... Shortly....'

And off she slipped down the corridors, leaving the
old servant alarmed. Something serious? What on
earth could there have been? A misfortune? But she
had nothing dearer in the world, nobody but this one
and only relative.

Then it must be to do with herself. But where was
she reproachable? What was the accusation? She'd
never cheated anyone out of a penny. When she went
to confession, she truly did not know what to say and
with what sin to charge herself.

Barbe remained thoroughly anxious. Sister Rosalie's
look had been so dark, her tone of voice almost severe.
The joyful day was all over. She no longer had the heart
to laugh, to mingle with the groups of people there who
were chatting away, making merry, examining the latest
examples of intricately patterned lacework.

Alone, seated to one side, she thought over the
unknown matter of which Sister Rosalie was going to
tell her.

After grace had been said, they sat down at table in
the long refectory. But Barbe, barely touching her
food and then without any pleasure, watched as the
healthy, rosy-cheeked nuns and a few other family
visitors like her did justice to this festive Sunday
dinner. On that day they served the unctuous, golden
sacramental wine of Tours. Thinking she might drown
her cares, Barbe emptied the glass she had been
served. But she felt a headache coming on.

The meal had seemed endless to her. As soon as it was finished, she ran straight to Sister Rosalie with a questioning look on her face. Rosalie noticed her uneasiness and tried quickly to calm her down.

'It's nothing, Barbe! Come, come, my friend, don't alarm yourself so!'

'What is it?'

'Nothing! Nothing very serious. I have to give you a piece of advice.'

'Oh! You frightened me....'

'When I say nothing serious I mean not at present. But the matter could become serious. Here it is: it may be necessary for you to find another job.'

'Find another job! Then why? I've been with M. Viane for five years. I'm attached to him because I've seen his unhappiness; and he relies on me. He's the most upright man in the world.'

Barbe had turned quite pale and asked:

'What are you trying to say? What has my master done wrong?'

Sister Rosalie then told her the whole story that had spread across town, even been divulged within the calm enclosure of the Beguinage: the misbehavior of the man whom everyone had formerly admired for his poignant and inconsolable grief. Well! He had consoled himself in a disgusting way! He was now going out with an ex-theater dancer, a woman of ill repute....

Barbe quaked with fear; at each and every word, she fought back an inner revulsion; for she revered her relative, and these so offensive and incredible revelations carried an authority coming from her mouth. So then, was that the cause of all that change in his life of which she understood nothing, the frequent sorties, the comings and goings, the meals out, the late returns, the nocturnal absences?....

The beguine continued:

'Barbe, have you considered that an honest Christian servant can no longer stay in the service of a man who has become a libertine?'

At that word Barbe exploded: it wasn't possible! Slanderous, all of it, and Sister Rosalie had been taken in. Such a good master, who adored his wife! He, who each morning still, under her very own eyes, went to cry over the portraits of the deceased one and kept her hair better than a holy relic.

'It's as I tell you,' replied Sister Rosalie calmly. 'I know everything. I even know this woman's house. It's on my way into town and more than once I've seen M. Viane going in or out.'

This was conclusive. Barbe seemed brought down. She said nothing in reply, lost in thought, a large furrow and wrinkles in the middle of her forehead.

Then she simply said, 'I'll consider,' while her relative, called back to her duties, left her for a moment.

The old servant remained stunned, weak, her mind confused by this news that was thwarting all her hopes and upsetting her future course in life.

First of all, she was attached to her master and it would be painful to leave him.

And then, what other job would she find, as good, as relatively easy and as well paid? In this bachelor household, she would have been able to save that small but crucial sum of money to secure the rest of her days in the Beguinage. Yet Sister Rosalie was right. She could no longer remain with a man involved in a moral scandal.

She knew already that one cannot remain in the service of an impious person, one who did not pray, did not observe Lent, the Ember Days or the laws of the Church. It was the same reason in the case of profligates. They commit the very worst sin, the guilt of which, say the preachers in sermons and retreats, threatens one most with the fires of hell. And Barbe quickly banished from her mind any distant association with lewdness, the very naming of which led her to cross herself.

What was she to decide? Barbe remained highly perplexed, throughout vespers and the solemn benediction, for the celebration of which she returned with the rest of the community to the church. She prayed fervently to the Holy Ghost for guidance; and her prayers were answered, for on leaving the church, she had made a decision.

Since it was a thorny matter and beyond her powers of judgment, she would go straight away to her regular confessor at Notre-Dame and humbly follow his judgment.

Barbe told the priest all she had just learned. He had known this simple, upright character for years, how quickly tormented by scruples she was, thanks to which her poor dark soul seemed truly crowned with thorns. He sought to calm her and made her promise not to be over hasty: if what they were saying about her master was true and he was thus guilty of such a liaison, there was still room for distinction in her case; insofar as the assignations had taken place outside the house, she had to ignore them, in any case not allow them to trouble her so; if, unfortunately, this wicked woman in question were to come to her master's house, to visit him, for dinner or anything else, she could, in that case, no longer be party to the profligacy, would have to hand in her notice and leave.

Barbe got him to repeat this distinction for her; then, having understood it, she came out of the confessional, left the church after a short prayer and made her way back towards the Quai du Rosaire, towards the home she had left so happily in the morning and which she sensed quite well she would sooner or later have to quit....

Ah! How hard it is to be joyful for long! And she went home by way of the dead streets, wishing it was still the green suburb of the dawn, the mass, the white canticles, everything upon which night was falling; thinking of imminent departures, of new faces, of her master in a state of mortal sin; and seeing herself henceforth without hope of ending her life in the Beguinage, dying on such an evening as this, all alone, in the hospice whose windows look out over the canal....

IX

Hugues had experienced a great disillusionment since the day he had that strange whim of putting Jane in one of his wife's old-fashioned dresses. He had gone too far. Through wanting to unite the two women, their resemblance had diminished. The delusion was possible so long as they remained far removed from each other, separated by the mist of death. Drawn too close together, the differences appeared.

In the beginning, thoroughly dazzled by the recovery of the same face, his emotion was an accessory; then, gradually, through wanting to break the parallel into tiny pieces, he came to torment himself over nuances.

The resemblances are never only in the figures and in the overall impression. If one strains over details, everything differs. Without realizing that he had himself changed his way of looking, comparing with more meticulous care, Hugues blamed Jane for it and believed her to be totally transformed in herself.

Certainly, she still had the same eyes. But, if the eyes are the windows of the soul, it is certain that another soul was emerging from them today than in those, always present, of the dead woman. Gentle and reserved to begin with, Jane was slowly letting herself go. A musty smell of the wings and the theater reappeared. Intimacy had given her freedom in her walk, a raucous and ungainly mirth, loose talk; and all day around the house, her old habit of slovenly dress returned, untidy in a peignoir and her hair a confused mass. Hugues's distinguished bearing took offence at it. However, he still went to her house, seeking to recapture the escaping mirage. Long drawn out hours! Cheerless evenings! He needed that voice. He still drank its dark flood. And at the same time he suffered from the spoken words.

For her part, Jane was tiring of his dark moods and lengthy silences. Now, when he arrived in the evenings, she was no longer there, staying late around the town, buying things in the shops, trying on dresses. He also came to see her at other times, in broad daylight, in the morning or the afternoon. Often she had gone out, not wanting to stay at home. Bored by her lodgings, always out and about in the streets. Where did she go? Hugues didn't know of her having any friends. He waited for her; he didn't like being alone, preferring to walk the neighborhood until she returned. Sad, anxious, fearing people's eyes, he walked aimlessly, adrift, from one sidewalk to the other, made for nearby quays, sauntered alongside the water, came to symmetrical squares made gloomy by moaning trees, dived into the endless tangle of grey streets.

Ah! Always that greyness of the streets of Bruges!

Hugues felt his soul coming more and more under this grey influence. He submitted to the contagion of this sparse silence, this emptiness without passers-by—apart from a few old women in black cloaks, heads buried beneath hoods who, similar to shadows, were returning from having been to light a candle in the chapel of the Holy Blood. Curious thing: one never sees so many old women as in the old cities. They trudge about, already the color of the earth, aged and silent, as if all their words were spent.... Hugues, walking haphazardly, barely noticed them, too engrossed in his former sorrow and his present worries. Mechanically, he came back to Jane's house. Still nobody!

He started to walk again, hesitated, set off again down the shrunken streets, arrived at the Quai du

Rosaire. Then he decided to return home; he would visit Jane later, in the evening; sat down in an armchair, tried to read; then, within seconds, drowned in solitude, overcome by the cold silence of those long hallways, he went out again.

It is the evening... it is drizzling, a light rain that draws out, grows heavier, pinning his soul.... Hugues was feeling reconquered, haunted by the face, pushed towards her abode. He made his way there, drew near, retraced his steps, gripped suddenly by a need for isolation, fearing now that she was waiting there for him and not wanting to see him.

He walked at a swift pace in the opposite direction, taking to old parts of the city, wandering he knew not where, vague, pitiful, in the mud. The rain grew faster, reeling off its threads, ravelling its cloth, drawing its stitches tighter, a wet, imperceptible net in which Hugues gradually felt himself weaken. He began again to remember... he thought of Jane. What was she doing, at such a time, outside in this desolate weather? He thought of his wife.... What had become of her too? Her poor grave... the wreaths and flowers ruined by these downpours....

And bells were ringing, so faint, so distant! How far away the city! One would think that in its turn it no longer existed, had been dissolved, drowned in the rain that submerged everything.... Matched sadness! It is for Bruges-la-Morte that a sound of parish bells still tumbles from the highest surviving belfries, and grieves!

X

As Hugues felt his touching falsity escaping him, so therefore he turned again towards the city, uniting his soul with it, straining for that other parallel with which he had previously—when first a widower and newly arrived in Bruges—already filled his sorrow. Now that Jane was ceasing to seem to him wholly like his wife, he began again to be similar to the city. He sensed it keenly on his monotonous and continual walks through the empty streets.

For he was growing incapable of staying at home, frightened by the solitude of the place, by the wind crying in the chimneys, by the memories multiplying around him there like so many staring eyes. He went out almost all day long, at random, all at sea, unsure of Jane and of his own feeling for her.

Did he really love her? And what indifference or betrayal might she herself be hiding? Sad, shortening ends of winter afternoons! Hanging, binding mist! He felt the contagious fog fill his very soul, and all his thoughts blurred and drowned in a grey lethargy.

Ah! This Bruges on a winter evening!

The influence of the city on him was beginning again: lesson in silence from the still canals, their calm ennobled by the presence of stately swans; example of resignation offered by the taciturn quays; above all, pious and austere advice tumbling from the tall belfries of Notre-Dame and Saint-Sauveur always looming in the background. He lifted his eyes to them instinctively as if to seek refuge there; but the towers derided his wretched love. They seemed to say: 'Look at us! We are nothing but faith! Cheerless, without sculpted smiles, with the look of citadels of the air, we climb towards God. We are the military towers. And the Devil has spent his arrows against us!'

Oh, yes! Hugues would have liked to be thus. Nothing but a tower, above life! But unlike these belfries of Bruges, he could not pride himself on having foiled the efforts of the Devil. On the contrary, people said that the overwhelming passion from which he suffered as one possessed was a malefice of the Devil!

Stories of satanism, things he had read, came back to him. Was there not some basis to these fears of witchcraft and occult powers?

And wasn't it like the sequel to a blood bond that would lead him to some catastrophe? At times, Hugues thus felt that the shadow of Death would draw near to him.

He had wanted to dodge, triumph over and flout death by the specious artifice of a resemblance. Death, perhaps, would gain its revenge.

But he could still escape, exorcize himself in time! And across parts of the great mystical city in which he wandered, he raised his eyes towards the merciful towers, the consolation of the bells, the compassionate welcome of the madonnas who, on every street corner, hold out their arms from within a niche, surrounded by candles and by roses under a globe, which one might say were dead flowers in a glass coffin.

Yes, he would throw off this evil yoke! He would repent. He had been the 'Unfrocked Priest of Sorrow.' But he would do penance. He would become again what he had been. Already he was beginning to be like the city again. He was finding himself again the brother in silence and melancholy of this mournful Bruges, this *soror dolorosa.* How right he had been to come there at the time of his great grief! Mute analogies! Reciprocal penetration of soul and material things! We enter into them, while they impregnate us.

Thus cities especially have a personality, an autonomous spirit, an almost externalized character corresponding to joy, to new love, to renunciation, to widowerhood. Every city is a state of mind, and one hardly needs to stay there for this state of mind to communicate itself, to spread to us in a fluid that inoculates and that one incorporates with the nuance of the air.

From the outset, Hugues had sensed this pale and soothing influence of Bruges, and by it he had resigned himself to the solitary memories, to the abeyance of hope, to the wait for sweet death....

And still now, in the evening, despite his present anguish, he could nonetheless feel his pain diluted a little in the canals of tranquil water, and he tried to make himself over in the image and likeness of the city.

XI

Now the city has above all a believer's face. Counsels of faith and renunciation emanate from it, from its convent and hospice walls, from its frequent churches kneeling in tunics of stone. It was beginning to control Hugues again and to impose its obedience. It was again becoming a person, the principal interlocutor in his life, making an impression, dissuading, ordering, according to whom one finds one's bearings and all one's reasons for action.

Hugues soon found himself again won over by this mystical side of the city, now that he was beginning to escape from the form of sex and falsehood in woman. He was listening less to that; and, correspondingly, he heard the bells more and more.

Numerous, tireless bells while again he took, during relapses into sadness, to going out at dusk, to wandering aimlessly along the quays.

He was pained by those permanent bells—toll of the requiem, obit or thirty masses; call to matins and vespers—out of view, all day long swinging their black censers, whence puffed out a kind of smoke of sound.

Those uninterrupted bells of Bruges, that great death knell intoned without respite in the air! How a disgust with life came from it, a clear sense of the vanity of all things and the reminder of our death on its way....

In the empty streets, where every now and then a street lamp keeps life going, rare silhouettes were few and far between, common women in their long black cloaks like bells of bronze, swaying like them. And in a parallel direction, the cloaks and the bells seemed to be following an identical route towards the churches.

Hugues felt unconsciously advised. He followed in their wake. The encompassing fervor had won him over again. The propaganda of example, the latent will of things was drawing him back in turn into the contemplation of the old churches.

As in the beginning, he took again to stopping there in the evenings, especially in those naves of Saint-Sauveur with their long black marbles and the rococo rood-loft, whence now and then tumbles forth music that shimmers and unfurls....

This music was vast, ran down pipes onto the flagstones; and that, one would have said, is what drowned and erased the dusty inscriptions on the tombstones and brasses scattered all over the basilica. It could truly be said that there one walked in death!

So nothing—neither the gardens of stained glass windows, nor the wonderful, ageless paintings by Pourbus, Van Orley, Quellin, De Crayer and Seghers, framed by garlands of never-fading tulips—could mitigate the tomb-like sadness of the place. And even in the triptychs and altar screens, Hugues could barely contemplate the enchanting colors and this eternalized dream of far-off painters, without dreaming with greater melancholy of death, while seeing, on the panels, the clasped hands of the donor and the cornelian eyes of the donatrix—of whom nothing remains but these portraits! Then he called the dead woman to mind again—he no longer wished to think about the living woman, that lascivious Jane whose image he left at the church door—it's with the dead woman that he also dreamed of kneeling in the presence of God, like the pious donors of a short time ago.

In his times of spiritual crisis, Hugues still liked to go and bury himself in the silence of the little Jerusalem chapel. The cloaked women especially made their way there, at sundown.... He followed them in; the aisles were low; a kind of crypt. Right in the further-most part, in that chapel constructed in adoration of the Saviour's wounds, a life-size figure of Christ in the tomb, pale beneath a fine lace shroud. The cloaked women lit small candles, then moved away with glid-ing steps. And the candles bled a little. In that shadow, it seemed as if the holy wounds of Jesus were opening up, beginning to flow again, to wash away the sins of all those who came there.

But, among his pilgrimages across the city, Hugues especially adored L'Hôpital Saint-Jean, where the sublime Memling lived and left some pure master-pieces to tell, throughout the centuries, the fresh-ness of his convalescent dreams. Hugues also went there hoping to heal himself, to bathe his over-excited retina in those white walls. The great catechism of calm!

Box-trimmed inner gardens; in the background, secluded sickrooms where voices are kept low. A few nuns pass by, barely displacing a little silence, as the swans of the canals barely displace a little water. In the air hangs a scent of damp linen, of rainwashed coifs, of musty altar-cloths just removed from ancient cupboards.

Hugues finally arrived at the sanctuary of art, the room containing the unique paintings, where the famous Shrine of Sainte-Ursula shines, like a little Gothic chapel in gold, unfolding on each side, on three panels, the story of the eleven thousand virgins; while in the enamelled metal of the roof, in delicate miniature-like medallions, there are angelic musi-cians with violins the color of their hair and harps the shape of their wings.

Thus the martyrdom is accompanied by painted music. It is infinitely gentle, this death of the vir-gins, grouped like a mass of azaleas in the moored galley that is to become their tomb. The soldiers are on the bank. They have already begun the massacre; Ursula and her companions have disembarked. The blood flows—but so pink! The wounds are petals.... The blood doesn't drip; it sheds its petals on the breasts.

The virgins are happy and quite peaceful, catching sight of their courage in the gleaming mirrors of the soldiers' armor. And the death-delivering bow itself seems soft like the waxing of the moon!

By way of these subtle touches, the artist had expressed that the agony, for the faithful virgins, was only a transubstantiation, an experience willingly accepted on behalf of the imminent joy. That is why the peacefulness, already reigning within them, spreads out into the landscape, filling it up with their spirit as planned.

Transitory minute: it is less the slaughter than already the apotheosis; the drops of blood are beginning to congeal into rubies for eternal diadems; and heaven is opening up, its light is visible, taking over the sprinkled earth....

Angelic understanding of the martyrdom! Paradisal vision of a painter as pious as he was possessed of genius.

Hugues was moved. He dreamed of the faith of these great Flemish artists, who left us these truly votive pictures—those for whom painting was like prayer!

Thus with all these spectacles: the works of art and of gold, the architecture, the cloistered look of the houses, the miter-shaped gables, the streets adorned with madonnas, the wind full of the peal of bells, all crowded in on Hugues as an example of piety and austerity, the contagiousness of an inveterate Catholicism in the air and the stones.

At the same time, the extreme devoutness of his early childhood came back to him, bringing with it a nostalgia for innocence. He felt a little guilty towards God, as much as towards his wife. The idea of sin was reappearing, emerging.

Especially since one Sunday evening, when chancing to enter the cathedral for the evening service and the organ music, he had been present at the end of a sermon.

The priest spoke on the theme of death. And what other subject to choose but that, in the gloomy city, where it presents and imposes itself, and alone makes its vine of black grapes climb around the pulpit, up to the hand of the preacher who has only to pluck them. What to speak of, if not of that which is everywhere in the atmosphere there: the inevitability of death! And what other thought to study than that of one's soul to save, which is the main worry here and the constant pang of consciences.

Now the priest, airing his views on death, the good death that was only a passage, and also on the reunion of the saved souls in God, spoke as well of that most dangerous sin, that mortal sin, that is to say the one that makes death a true death, without deliverance or recovery of loved ones.

Close to a pillar, Hugues listened, not without a little emotion. The great church was shadowy, barely lit by a few lamps and candles. The faithful huddled together in a mass of black, almost incorporated by the shadow. It seemed to him that he was alone, that the priest was facing him, addressing him. By a strange coincidence or by the activities of his imagination, it was as if the general address was a discussion of his own case. Yes! He was in a state of sin! He had vainly tried to delude himself over his guilty love and invoke this justification of resemblance with regard to it. He was carrying out the work of the flesh. He was doing that which the Church always reproved most severely: he was living in a kind of concubinage.

Now, if religion tells the truth, if saved Christians find one another again, he would never see her again, that saintly and missed one, for not having desired her exclusively. Death would only eternalize the absence, consecrate a separation he had believed to be temporary.

Afterwards, like now, he would live far away from her; truly his eternal torment would be to remember her always in vain.

Hugues left the church deeply disturbed. And, from that day on, the thought of sin went round and round in his mind, drove in its nail. He would have liked to be rid of it, be absolved. The thought of confessing came to him, of halting his distress, the capsizing of his soul down into which he was slipping. But he had to repent, to change his ways; and, in spite of the grievances, his daily suffering caused by Jane, he no longer felt strong enough to leave her and return to being alone.

Yet the city, with its believer's face, reproached, insisted. It put forward the model of its own chastity, its strict faith....

And the bells connived in this, while now each evening he wandered with growing anguish, with the pain of loving Jane and missing his wife, of fearing his sinfulness and possible damnation.... At first friendly, the bells offered good advice; but soon they ceased to commiserate, chiding him—visible and palpable around him, so to speak, like the jackdaws around towers—jostling him, entering his head, assaulting him and doing him violence, in order to pick off his wretched love and to pluck out his sin!

XII

Hugues was suffering; from day to day the dissimilarities grew more marked. It was no longer even possible for him to deceive himself over the outward appearance. Jane's face had taken on a certain hardness, as well as a weariness, a furrow under the eyes which cast a kind of shadow over the still identical pearl and the jet-black pupil. She had also taken again to the fancy, as in her theatrical days, of softening the cheeks with powder, of coloring the mouth, of blackening the eyebrows.

Hugues had tried vainly to dissuade her from using this make-up, so out of tune with the chaste, natural face he remembered. Jane scoffed, ironical, hard, overwrought. Mentally, he then called to mind the gentleness of the dead woman, her good humor, her words of such tender nobleness, like petals falling from her mouth. Ten years of life together without a quarrel, without one of those black words that rise like the slime of the stirred-up depth of a soul.

The difference between the two women now grew more specific each day. Oh, no! The dead woman was not like that! This evidence grieved him deeply, putting an end to what had been the excuse for what he began to see was a wretched adventure. An embarrassment, almost a shame, overcame him: he no longer dared dream of her for whom he had cried so and in respect of whom he began to feel guilty.

He rarely entered any longer those rooms of her eternalized memories, troubled, confused by the look of her portraits, a look—one would have said—of reproach. And the tress of hair continued to rest in the almost forsaken glass case, where the dust built up its little grey ash.

More than ever, he felt his soul quite weak and crippled: going out, coming back, going out again, chased—so to speak—from his house to Jane's, attracted by her face when he was far from it, and beset by regrets, remorse and self-contempt when he found himself at her side.

His household was in confusion too; no longer any punctuality or organization. He gave orders, then changed them; cancelled his meals. Old Barbe no longer knew how to arrange her housework or her shopping. Sad, worried, knowing the cause, she prayed to God for her master....

Bills often arrived, receipts, claiming large sums of money for purchases made by this woman. Receiving them in her master's absence, Barbe remained astounded: endless clothes, baubles, incredibly expensive jewels, all manner of things obtained on credit, using and abusing her lover's name, in the city shops where she bought incessantly, with a prodigality that mocked expenditure.

Hugues gave in to all her whims. However, she wasn't in the least bit grateful. More and more, she stepped up her outings, occasionally absenting herself for a whole day and evening too; postponing her rendezvous with Hugues, writing him hurried notes.

She pretended now to have established a few relations. She had friends. Was she always to live alone like that? On another occasion, she informed him that her sister in Lille was ill. She'd never spoken to him of this relative before but now she had to go to see her. She stayed away for a few days. When she returned, the same stratagems began again: disordered life, absences, outings, to-and-fro of a fan, flux and reflux on which Hugues's own existence found itself hanging.

In the long run, he grew a little suspicious; he kept an eye on her; went to prowl around her house in the evening, nocturnal ghost in this sleeping Bruges. He knew the hidden lookouts, the breathless halts, the sudden rings of the doorbell whose titillation dies in the passages that stay silent, the watch outdoors until late at night in front of a lighted window, the screen of a blind where a silhouette—that one believes at each second to be two silhouettes—moves in shadow play.

He no longer concerned himself with the dead woman; Jane's charm had gradually bewitched him and he trembled at the thought of losing her. It was no longer just her face, it was her flesh, her whole body, whose burning image called itself forth from the other side of night, while he could only make out its floating shadow in the folds of the curtains.... Yes! He did love her, since he was jealous to the point of suffering, of crying, when in the evening he kept watch on her, stung by the midnight carillons, by the fine rain, incessant in this North, where the clouds fray into unrelieved drizzle.

And he remained, always lying in wait, going to-and-fro in a small area as in a courtyard, speaking vague words out loud like a sleepwalker, in spite of the rain getting heavier—slush, mud, heavy skies, late winter, all the desolate sadness of things....

He would have liked to know, elucidate, see.... Oh! What anguish! What soul, then, did this woman have to hurt him so, while the other—the one so good, the dead one—seemed in these supreme minutes of his distress to rise in the night and look at him with the pitying eyes of the moon.

Hugues was not fooled; he had caught Jane lying, had put two and two together; soon he was fully informed when, as is customary in these provincial cities, letters rained down on him, anonymous cards full of sarcastic and vindictive remarks, details of cheating, of the licentious behavior he had already suspected.... He was furnished with names, with evidence. So there was the outcome of this affair with a pick-up in which a cause, so honorable at first, had led him astray. As for her, he would break off; that's all! But how would he put right his own fall from grace, his grief made ridiculous, this sacred thing—his cult and his sincere despair—that had become the butt of public derision?

Hugues was distressed. Jane too was finished for him; it was like the death of his wife a second time. Oh! All he had put up with from this capricious, unfaithful woman!

One last evening he went to her house determined to rid himself, by saying goodbye, of the weight of sorrow piled upon his soul on her account.

Without anger, with an immeasurable heartbreak, he told her he had learned everything; and as she took it haughtily, badly, with a show of courage: 'What? What are you saying?' he showed her the damning reports, the shameful documents....

'Are you fool enough to believe anonymous letters?' And she started to laugh cruelly, showing her teeth made for preying on victims.

'Your own wiles had already enlightened me,' observed Hugues.

Jane, suddenly furious, came and went, causing the doors to slam as she swished the air with her skirt.

'Well, what if it is true?' she explained. Then, a moment later: 'Besides, I've had enough of living here! I'm leaving.'

Hugues had watched her while she was speaking. In the bright lamplight, he saw again her clear face, her black pupils, her false dyed golden hair, false like her heart and her love! No! Her face was no longer that of the dead woman; but she, shaking in that pei-gnoir in which her throat was pulsating, was certainly the woman he had embraced; and, on hearing her cry 'I'm leaving!' his whole soul capsized, turned back towards an infinity of shadow....

In that solemn moment, he felt that after the illu-sions of the mirage and the resemblance, he had also loved her sensually—belated passion, sad October inflamed by a chance of late-blooming roses!

All his ideas whirled round in his head; he only knew one thing: he was suffering, he was in pain, and he wouldn't suffer any more if Jane didn't threaten to leave. Such as she was, he still wanted her. Inside he was ashamed of his cowardice; but he couldn't live on without her.... Besides, who knows? The world is so unkind! She had not even wanted to vindicate herself.

Then he was suddenly struck by an immense anguish at this end of a dream that he felt acutely (the ruptures of love are like a little death, having also their departures without farewells). But it was not just the separation from Jane, nor the broken mirror of reflections, that grieved him most deeply at that moment: he felt especially a terrible thought of the threat of renewed solitude—face to face with the city—without anyone between the city and himself. Yes, indeed, he had chosen it, this irremediable Bruges and its grey melancholy.

But the weight of the shadow of the towers was too heavy.

And Jane had made him accustomed to feel the shadow over his soul arrested by her. Now he would succumb to it all. He was going to be alone again, prey to the bells! More alone, as in a second widowerhood! The city, too, would seem more deathly to him.

Hugues, distraught, rushed towards Jane, grabbed her hand and begged: 'Stay! Stay! I was crazy...' his voice weak, wet with tears—so to speak—as if he had cried within.

That evening, coming home along the quays, he felt uneasy, dreading some unknown danger. Gloomy thoughts assailed him. The dead woman haunted him. She seemed to have returned, drifting in the distance, enshrouded in the fog. Hugues judged himself more guilty than ever with respect to her. Suddenly, a wind blew up. The poplars on the bank were complaining. On the canal alongside him a stirring disturbed the swans, those beautiful secular swans of a hundred years' standing, swans of expiation, that the city was bound to look after indefinitely, for having unjustly put to death a knight whose coat of arms had depicted them and from which—so goes the legend—they were descended.

Normally so calm and white, the swans now took fright, ruffling the watery silk of the canal, excitable, restless, surrounding one of their number that was beating its wings and then, leaning on the others, was rising up from the water, like a sick person struggling to get out of his bed.

The bird seemed to be suffering: at intervals it cried; then, raising itself into flight, its cry grew softer and more distant; it was a wounded voice, almost human in its varying pitch and tone....

Hugues watched, listened, troubled by this mysterious scene. He recalled the popular belief. Yes! The swan was singing! It was about to die, then, or at least sensed death in the air!

Hugues shuddered. Was this an ill omen for him? The painful scene with Jane, her threat to leave, had prepared him only too well for these dark forebodings. What again would be the outcome of all this? For what mourning were these crapes of the superstitious night? Of what will he be widower again?

XIII

Jane took advantage of the grave situation. That day, with her flair for being an adventuress, she had understood what power she had taken over this man, quite infected by her, malleable to her will.

With a few words she had completely succeeded in reassuring him, in reconquering him, in reenthroning herself undamaged in his eyes. Then she had calculated that at his age, burdened with long sorrows, ill as he was, so changed already in the course of the last few months, Hugues would not live long. Now he was reputed to be rich; he was a stranger and alone in that city, knowing no one there. What madness for her to consider letting go of the inheritance she could so easily secure!

Jane quietened down a little, coming and going less frequently and more convincingly, taking only discreet risks.

One day she felt a desire to go into Hugues's house, that vast ancient place on the Quai du Rosaire, affluent-looking, with impenetrable lace curtains, tattoos of hoarfrost sticking to the window panes, permitting no conjecture as to what lay behind.

Jane would have very much liked to enter his house, assess his probable fortune by his material wealth, inspect his furniture, his jewellery and silverware, everything she coveted, to make a mental note of which possessions she would decide to acquire.

But Hugues had never agreed to receive her there.

Jane turned on her winning ways again. It was like a renewal between them, a relaxed and agreeable lull. Precisely the right moment presented itself: it was May; on the following Monday was the procession of the Holy Blood, the centuries-old annual excursion of the shrine that preserves a drop of blood from the spear wound of Christ.

The procession would make its way along the Quai du Rosaire, under Hugues's windows. Jane had never been present at the famous procession and showed her curiosity about it. Now it would not go past her own house, which was too far away; and how would she see it in the crowded streets, since it was said that, on the day, people would flock from all over Flanders.

'Look! How about it? I'll come to your house.... We'll have dinner together....'

Hugues protested that the neighbors and servants would gossip.

'I'll come early, when everyone is asleep.'

He was also worried in thinking about Barbe, so prudish and devout, who would take her for a devil's messenger.

But Jane insisted: 'Well then! Agreed?'

And her voice was cajoling; it was the voice from the beginning of their affair, that tempting voice possessed by all women at certain times, a crystal voice that sings, swells into haloes, in eddies where men surrender, whirl round and let themselves go.

XIV

Barbe rose very early that Monday, much earlier than usual, for she had only part of the morning to prepare the house for the passing of the procession.

She went to the first mass at five thirty, took communion ardently, then returned home to begin the preparations. The silver candlesticks were brought out of the cupboards along with silver vases and chafing-dishes in which to burn incense. Barbe rubbed and polished each object until the metal shone like mirrors. She also got out the finest cloths to set on little tables she placed in front of each window, a kind of temporary resting place, attractive altars for the May devotions to the Virgin Mary, on each of which she set a candlelit crucifix and a statuette of the Blessed Virgin....

She had also to consider the external decorations, for on this particular day each person competes with the next in pious zeal. Now, according to custom, the house fronts had already been decorated with greeny-bronze pine boughs offered from door to door by peasants, and which formed a double row of trees lining the streets.

On the balcony, in an adornment of chaste folds, Barbe arranged papal-coloured draperies and white fabrics. Nimble and busy, she came and went ingratiatingly, handling respectfully this annual decorative ritual, which for her partook of the saintliness of the occasion, as if priests' fingers, ingrained with holy oils, had consecrated these things with an untransferable holy water. She seemed to herself to be in a sacristy.

She had only then to fill the baskets with herbs and cut flowers—loose mosaic, crumbled carpet with which each servant colors the street in front of her house as the procession passes by. Barbe made haste, slightly tipsy from the scent of hollyhocks, huge lilies, daisies, sage, aromatic rosemary and reeds that she cut into short ribbons. And her hand dipped into the baskets, filling up, refreshed by this massacre of petals, fresh waddings, quilts of dead wings.

Through the open windows came the swelling concert of the parish bells that sounded forth one after another.

The weather was grey, one of those undecided May days when, despite the clouds, there is a kind of after-joy in the sky. And on account of this delicacy in the air, from which one guessed each new peal of bells, a cheerfulness spread from it to her; and the aged bells, the played out ones, the grandmothers on crutches, those of the convents, of the old towers, those stay-at-homes, those valetudinarians who stay quiet all year, but come out to take their places on the day of the Holy Blood procession—all seemed, beneath their worn bronze dresses, to wear bright white surplices, crimped underwear in fan folds. Barbe listened to the ringing, the great cathedral bell heard only on important holidays, slow and black, striking the silence like a crosier.... And also all the small bells from nearby turrets—agitation, merry tinkling of silver dresses, also apparently organizing themselves into procession in the sky....

Barbe's piety was growing in enthusiasm; that morning, it seemed that a fervor was in the air, that a heavenly ecstasy showered its petals with the full peal of the bells, that one heard invisible wings, a procession of angels.

And all of that seemed to converge on her soul, her soul where she felt the presence of Jesus, where the host, that she had incorporated at the dawn mass, was shining, still whole, in a perfect sphere in whose center she saw a face.

The old servant, dreaming again of the goodness of Jesus that was truly within her, crossed herself, began to pray again, having the remembrance and the savor of the Blessed Sacrament in her mouth.

However, her master had rung for her; it was his lunchtime. He took the opportunity to inform her that he was expecting someone for dinner and that she should make the appropriate arrangements.

Barbe was astounded; he had never received anyone! That struck her as strange; suddenly a ghastly thought crossed her mind. What if that which she had formerly feared was going to happen?—that which she no longer thought about, because she had become a little reassured—she had guessed it!... yes! It was that woman, that one of whom Sister Rosalie had spoken to her, who perhaps was going to come....

Barbe felt her blood run cold.... In that case, her mind was made up, her duty clear: to open the door to that creature, serve her at table, follow her instructions, associate with sinfulness—had been strictly forbidden her by her confessor. And on such a day! A day when the very blood of Jesus was going to pass in front of the house! And she, who had taken communion that morning!... Oh! No! It was impossible! She would have to hand in her notice at once.

She wanted to know and, with the petty tyranny which comes easily to servants of elderly bachelors or widowers in these quiet provinces, she hinted:

'Whom has Monsieur invited to dinner?'

Hugues replied that it was a little forward of her to interrogate him thus but that she would know when the person arrived.

But Barbe, dominated by her notion that seemed more and more likely to her, seized with fear and now with real panic, decided to risk everything in order not to be caught unawares, and she resumed:

'Isn't it perhaps a lady Monsieur is expecting?'

'Barbe!' said Hugues, astonished and a little severely, looking at her.

But she didn't falter:

'It's that I must know in advance. For if Monsieur *is* expecting a lady, I must beg to inform Monsieur that I shall be unable to serve him dinner.'

Hugues was stunned: was he dreaming? Was she going out of her mind?

But Barbe, strong, repeated that she was going to leave; she couldn't continue; she had already been forewarned; her confessor had ordered her to leave. She was not about to disobey, obviously, and put herself in a state of mortal sin—to die a sudden death and descend to hell.

At first Hugues understood nothing; bit by bit he unravelled the hidden thread, the likely gossip, word of the adventure put around. So, even Barbe knew too? And she was threatening to go away because Jane was coming? Then wasn't that woman to be totally despised, if his humble servant, bound to him for years by habit, by his interest, by the thousand threads that are woven daily between two coexistences, preferred to break off and leave him rather than serve her for one day?

Hugues remained weak and dumbfounded, his buoyant mood broken before this sudden crisis which was ruining his genial plans for that day in such an unforeseen way and, with a resigned air, he said simply:

'Well, Barbe, you may leave immediately.'

The old servant considered this and all of a sudden the good common soul, fully moved to pity, understanding that he was suffering, shook her head and, in that soft voice which Nature had bestowed upon her for lulling babies to sleep, she murmured:

'Oh! Jesus! My poor Monsieur!... And for a woman like that, a bad woman... who cheats you....'

Thus for a minute, forgetting the social distances, she had become motherly, ennobled by divine pity, her gushing cry like a spring that bathes and can heal....

But Hugues made her shut up, irritated and humiliated by this interference, by this audacity in speaking to him of Jane, and in what terms! It is he who was giving her leave, and without delay. She could come for her things the following day. But she should go today, she should go immediately!

Her master's annoyance took away the final scruples Barbe would have had in leaving him abruptly. She put on her fine black hooded cloak, pleased with herself and her self-sacrifice to duty, to Jesus who was within her....

Then calmly, unemotionally, she left the house that had been her home for five years; but before going on her way she strewed, in front of the house, the contents of the baskets she had emptied into her apron so that the street, at this spot only, would not be without its blaze of petals beneath the feet of the holy procession.

XV

How the day had started badly! One would think that all our joyful plans are like a challenge! Prepared too lengthily, they give time for fate to change the eggs in the nest, and we have to brood on sorrows.

Hearing the door of the house slam behind Barbe, Hugues experienced a distressing sensation. One more problem, a greater solitude, since the old servant had gradually become part of his life. All that on account of Jane, that cruel, inconsistent woman. Oh! What hadn't he suffered already on her account?

Now he really wished that she wouldn't come. He felt sad, anxious and irritable. He dreamed of the dead woman.... How had he been able to believe the lie of that quickly spoiled resemblance? And beyond the grave, what must she be thinking of the arrival of another in the home still filled with her presence, of Jane sitting in the armchairs where she had sat, of Jane superimposing, in the flow of the mirrors where the face of the dead continues to exist, her face on her own?

The bell rang. Hugues was forced to go open the door himself. It was Jane, late and flushed from her brisk walk. Brusque and imperious, she entered, taking in at a glance the great hallway, the drawing-rooms with open doors.

One could already hear echoes of distant music growing louder. The procession would not be long in coming.

Hugues himself had lit candles on the window ledges, on the small tables set out by Barbe.

He and Jane went up to the first floor and into his bedroom. The casement windows were closed. Jane went forward and opened one up.

'Oh! No!' said Hugues.

'Why?'

He pointed out to her that she couldn't let herself be seen like that, to attract attention to his house. Especially for the passing of a procession. The province is prudish. A scandal would ensue.

Jane had taken off her hat in front of the mirror; powdered her face a little with the puff from a small ivory case she always carried with her.

Then she returned to the casement, her hair uncovered and bright, its copper gleam catching the eye.

The crowd filling the street looked up curiously at this extraordinary woman flaunting her hair and clothing.

Hugues grew impatient. One could see enough from behind the curtains. He lurched forward and slammed the window shut.

Then Jane took offence, no longer wanted to watch, lay down on a sofa, hard and inscrutable.

The procession sang out. One heard it was getting nearer from the stretched moire of the canticles. Deeply hurt, Hugues had turned away from Jane; he rested his burning brow on the glass pane, freshness of water to dilute all his sorrow.

The first choirboys, singers with short cropped hair, passed by, chanting and carrying candles.

Hugues could clearly see the cortege through the window pane, in which the members of the procession stood out like the robes painted in the background of religious pictures in lace.

The body of worshippers walked past bearing pedestals with statues, with sacred hearts; holding up stiff golden banners like stained glass windows; then the pure white groups, the verger in robes, the archipelago of muslin from which incense puffed out in little blue waves—council of innocent children around a paschal lamb, white like them as if made of woolen snow.

Hugues turned momentarily towards Jane who, still sulking, remained slumped on the sofa, giving the impression of toying with cruel thoughts.

The solemn music of the serpents and ophicleides rose to mock the fragile, intermittent garland of the song of the sopranos.

And, through the window, Hugues's eyes met the knights of the Holy Land, the armored crusaders in golden brocade, the princesses of historic Bruges, all those who are linked to the name of Thierry of Alsace, bringer of the Holy Blood from Jerusalem. Now it was the young offspring of the noblest Flemish aristocrats who took these parts, wearing ancient materials, rare lace, age-old family jewels. It seemed as if the saints, warriors and donors of Van Eyck's and Memling's paintings had sprung back to life miraculously from their eternal places in the museums.

Utterly distressed by Jane's resentment, Hugues hardly watched, feeling immeasurably sad, even sadder during those canticles that pained him. He tried to pacify her. At his first word, her mood grew more antagonistic.

And she turned her eyes towards him, bristling, like hands full of things that were going to wound him all the more.

Silent and heartbroken, Hugues retired within himself, casting his soul, so to speak, to the swell of that music swirling through the streets, so that it would sweep him far from himself.

Then it was the turn of the clergy, the monks of every order to make their way forward: Dominicans, Redemptorists, Franciscans, Carmelites; then the seminarists in pleated tunics, sight-reading their antiphonaries; then the priests of each parish in their red choristers' outfits: vicars, curates, canons, in chasubles and embroidered dalmatics, shining like gardens of precious stones.

Wearing his miter, the bishop appeared beneath a canopy, bearing the shrine—a miniature gold cathedral topped by a cupola where, among a thousand cameos, diamonds, emeralds, amethysts, enamels, topaz and fine pearls, the unique ruby dreams from the chapel of the Holy Blood.

Won over by this mystical sensation, by the fervor of all these faces, by the faith of this vast crowd massing in the street beneath his windows, beyond, everywhere, right to the end of the city in prayer, Hugues also bowed his head when he saw everyone fall to their knees in submission on the blast of the canticles announcing the approach of the shrine.

Hugues had almost forgotten the reality, the presence of Jane, the latest scene that had put another block of ice between them. Seeing him moved, she sneered.

He pretended not to notice it, restraining an upsurge of hatred that he was beginning in fits and starts to feel for this woman.

Haughty, icy, she put on her hat, looking as if she was getting ready to leave. Hugues dared not break the heavy silence that had befallen the bedroom in the wake of the procession. The street had quickly emptied and was already silent with the excessive sadness of a passing joy.

Without a word she went downstairs; then, on the ground floor, as if having thought better of it or been seized by curiosity, she looked from the doorstep at the rooms whose doors had been left open. Taking several steps, she went straight into those two huge interconnected rooms, as if rebuked by the severity of their appearance. Rooms too have a physiognomy, a face. There are both immediate friendships and aversions between them and us. Jane felt unwelcome, out of the ordinary, out of place, out of sympathy with the mirrors, hostile towards the old furniture whose fixed, unchanging attitudes were threatened by her presence.

Tactlessly, she looked everything over.... She noticed here and there, on the walls and pedestal tables, the drawings and the photographs of Hugues's wife.

'Oh! So you've got pictures of women here?' And she let out a little malicious laugh.

She had approached the mantelpiece:

'Look here! One even looks like me....'

And she picked up one of the portraits.

Watching her uneasily as she moved about, Hugues suddenly felt sharply pained by the unwittingly cruel joke, the horrible jesting that was grazing the saintliness of the dead woman.

'Leave that alone!' he said in a voice that had become urgent.

Failing to understand, Jane burst out laughing.

Hugues advanced, took the portrait from her hands, shocked by these profane fingers on his mementos. He always handled them tremblingly, like the objects of a cult, like a priest with monstrance and chalice. His sorrow had become a religion to him. And, at this moment, the candles, not yet extinguished, that had been burning on the window ledges for the procession, lit up the drawing-rooms like chapels.

Jane, sarcastic, taking a perverse delight in Hugues's irritation, and secretly wishing to flout him even more, had moved into the other room, touching everything, upsetting the curios, rumpling the fabrics. Suddenly she stopped with a resounding laugh.

She had spotted the precious glass case on the piano and, to continue the effrontery, lifting the lid, pulled out the long tress of hair, unravelling it and waving it in the air, quite amazed and entertained.

Hugues had grown livid. This was profanation.... He had the impression of a sacrilege.... For years he had not dared touch that dead thing, since it was from a death. And that whole cult of the relic, with so many tears granulating the crystal each day, was serving finally as a plaything for a woman who scoffed at it.... Oh! How she had made him suffer more than enough for a long time! All his rancor, the flood of sufferings, drunk and filtered through every second of the hours for months, the suspicions, the betrayals, the waiting beneath her windows in the rain—all came back to him at once.... He was going to drive her out!

As he sprang forward, Jane took refuge behind the table, as in a game, defying him, suspending the tress from a distance, lowering it towards her face and mouth as if it was a charmed snake, winding it round her neck, a boa fashioned from the plumes of a golden bird....

'Give it to me! Give it to me!' shouted Hugues.

Jane ran to the right, then to the left, whirling around the table.

In the heat of this chase, intensified by Jane's sarcastic laughter, Hugues lost his head. He caught up with her. The hair still around her neck, she struggled fiercely, not wanting to yield it, now angry and cursing him for hurting her with the tight grip of his fingers.

'Will you?'

'No!' she replied, still laughing nervously beneath his grip.

Then Hugues went crazy; a flame sang in his ears; blood stung his eyes; a dizziness swept through his head, a sudden frenzy, a tightening of the fingertips, a desire to seize, to wring something, to snap flowers, a sensation of vice-like strength in his hands—he had grabbed the tress of hair that was still wound around Jane's neck, he wanted to recapture it! And wild, savage-looking, he pulled the tress until, taut, it was tight as a rope around her neck.

Jane no longer laughed; she had let out a little cry, a sigh, like the puff of a bubble expiring at water-level. Strangled, she fell to the ground.

....

She was dead—for having failed to guess the mystery and that one thing there was not to be touched on pain of sacrilege. She had laid a hand on the revengeful hair, that hair which, as emblem—for those whose soul is pure and in communion with the mystery—implied that the minute it was profaned, it would itself become *the instrument of death.*

Thus really the whole house had perished: Barbe had left; Jane lay dead; the dead woman was even further from him in death....

As for Hugues, he looked without understanding, without knowing anything more....

The two women had been identified as one alone. So similar in life, all the more so in death which had lent them a common pallor, he could no longer tell one from the other—single face of his love. Jane's corpse was the ghost of the former dead woman, visible there to him and him alone.

His soul retrogressing, Hugues could only recall very distant things, the beginnings of his widowerhood, back to which he believed himself to have returned.... Very calm, he found himself seated in an armchair.

The windows had remained open....

And, in the silence, came a sound of bells, all the bells at once, ringing again for the return of the procession to the chapel of the Holy Blood. Finished, the fine procession... all that had been, had sung—show of life, resurrection of a morning. The streets were empty again. The city was about to return to its solitude.

Hugues repeated incessantly, *'Morte... morte... Bruges-la-Morte,'* with a mechanical look, in a slack voice, trying to match *'Morte... morte... Bruges-la-Morte'* to the cadence of the last bells: slow, small, exhausted old women who seemed languishingly—is it over the city, is it over a tomb?—to be shedding petals of flowers of iron!